THE
ECOWARRIORS

To wondrous generous Leigh,
We'll keep it evergreen!
xoxo
Sandy

THE ECOWARRIORS

BOOK ONE:
THE BLUFFS OF BARABOO

SANDRA DREIS

iUniverse®

THE ECOWARRIORS
BOOK ONE: THE BLUFFS OF BARABOO

This is a work of fiction. All of the characters, names, incidents, organizations, and dialogue in this novel are either the products of the author's imagination or are used fictitiously.

Although characters and places are used fictitiously, sand mining and fracking, two highly controversial practices, are very real, indeed.

iUniverse books may be ordered through booksellers or by contacting:

iUniverse
1663 Liberty Drive
Bloomington, IN 47403
www.iuniverse.com
1-800-Authors (1-800-288-4677)

ISBN: 978-1-4917-7534-9 (sc)
ISBN: 978-1-4917-7533-2 (e)

Library of Congress Control Number: 2015953735

Print information available on the last page.

iUniverse rev. date: 10/23/2015

In memory of my father, David;

for my mother, Harriet,
heart of gold;

for my daughter, Haley,
my jet stream;

for my beloved family,
my treasure;

for the one and only Earth,
my home.

CONTENTS

PROLOGUE
BADGER AND MOTH

A luna moth. A badger. A budding astronomer and an old geologist. Uniquely different, but of one mind, they will answer the call of the earth. This very night, the presence of four ancient stones will be made known along the bluffs of Baraboo. The wind will carry the scent of a secret, an ancient secret finally unearthed like a letter unsealed. Insects, animals, even human beings will sense it, will hear the summons. Silt disturbed on a lake bottom. Stones revealed. A spiral carved into ice. All of this, a call to action. A crisis felt deep in the sap of evergreens. In the dry limbs of dormant oaks. By Roznos Meadow and Parfrey's Glen. By Green Lake and Eau de Claire. In the limestone cliffs and underground burrows.

An uncontrollable monster has come to Wisconsin—a sand monster that ravages, that will not be stopped. And here, among bluffs more than a billion years old, there is rebellion in soil, claw, and river rock. For in every direction, sand-mining pits scar the natural landscape, casting somber shadows over pristine meadows. Summer solstice, unable to hide the ugly mining pits, has come and gone, along with its luminous shades of vibrant green. The orange owl eyes, the yellow eyes of the wolf, the small black badger eyes—they see the same changes. Eyefuls of humiliation; desecration of natural beauty. Mountaintop removal wounds the horizon.

Fall came. Even the autumnal equinox—with its fiery display of burnt orange, yellow, and red—tried but could not conceal the sadly carved and barren patches of earth laden with machinery. And now, as the winter solstice approaches and arctic winds descend along the Baraboo River, a battle is about to begin. Wisconsin will be at war.

Devil's Lake holds the secret. Make no mistake; this Ice Age fortress remains securely guarded. Here, badgers rule. Ringing the pristine lake cut by the Wisconsin Glacier, five-hundred-foot cliffs have alluring but treacherous outcroppings, dramatic views, and deadly drops. Through seasons and solstices, water levels rise and fall. Sailboats and rowboats glide; augers drill for ice fishing. There are swimmers and floaters and those who squeeze pebbles between their toes. But beneath lapping water or quilt of ice, this lake bed has hidden and preserved the ancient treasure of Hermina. On the lake bottom, four stones of fantastical power and infinite mystery lie in sand. From Hermina, a royal badger, and an unknown luna moth, they lie in trust. A gift from one creature with infinite vision and one creature with invaluable wings, these stones endured through time—to the very present. In Wisconsin. In Baraboo. In a county named for the Sauk tribe.

Hermina, a revered badger queen and gifted seer, migrated from the flatlands of the Driftless area to the west. She came to a pristine lake, where she met her luna moth. For one fortunate moment, their destinies fused. Fortunate, because Hermina could foresee the future of Earth— not through her tiny badger eyes but through her earthbound instincts grounded deep in the soil. Thus, she saw the course, the patterns, the inevitable changes. At the same time, as summer ripened, the luna moth sensed its short life span coming to an end. Days were shortening; nights lengthening. The lime-green color of the luna's shapely wings enchanted Hermina. As the light of a full moon shone through the stained glass of the moth's lime-green scales, the badger was captivated; she saw the potential in them, the magic of their fragility. She understood their message, their significance. For the badger queen, the scales represented healing power.

And so, as the weary moth began to fade, Hermina envisioned a solution beneficial to both of them. The moth, suddenly too weak to fly, willingly agreed to exchange her dazzling green wings for immortality. When the moth expired, the badger blessed the delicate wings. She made a solemn promise of rebirth. Then the badger queen gently removed the precious green scales from each of the four wings. Meticulously, she mixed them into a gourd of pure liquid amber. Then, with utmost care, she strained the shimmering liquid through the fronds of a white ghost fern. When the distillation cooled, four gem-like stones were created. They were exquisite. Luminescent. More than jewels or precious ornaments, they sparkled with the intensity of life itself.

As Hermina had predicted, an energy source of immense power was created. A source not to be used—not right away. Rather, as the badger surmised, the stones were a kind of insurance to be preserved and kept safely until such power might be needed by future badger dynasties. Badger and moth. An alliance of earth and sky. Of creativity and sacrifice. For safekeeping, she buried the stones in a glacier-carved fortress: Devil's Lake. She chose a shallow but guarded spot not too far from shore. Here the walleye swam and darted between rocks and submerged tree limbs, outwitting frustrated anglers who fished from small wooden boats. The stones would rest in the sandy lake bed until they might be called upon for the good of all living things.

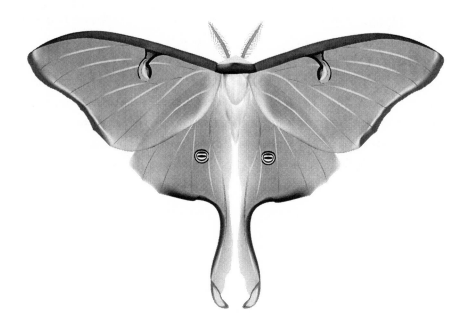

INTRODUCTION
THE MUSTA LUMINAE

The clear winter sky is alive with stars. Over central Wisconsin, the glimmering Winter Hexagon illuminates the ceiling of night. Six major constellations dangle their crystal lights. A celestial chandelier. From Auriga, the Charioteer, hangs the orb that sits highest in the sky, Capella, the she-goat. This bright yellow star reigns as the top vertex of the hexagon. Pastures and glens look up to her. Hills, bluffs, and even cliffs stand on tiptoe to compete with this daughter of mighty Auriga.

On the outskirts of the small city of Baraboo, streetlights are few. Only starlight enters the small upstairs window that faces the woods. Tonight, stargazing has been optimal for one young man, Davie Wyatt. His prized telescope sits upright like a giant praying mantis stalking the moon. His handsome face is hidden. Shoulder-length brown hair spreads in every direction as he lies facedown on a crushed pillow. Instead of pajamas, a Wisconsin Badgers sweatshirt and worn jeans cover his slender but wiry body. One arm dangles over the edge of the bed. As if flying atop a meteor shower, the other arm stretches forward on a star-patterned navy quilt. It is late. Very late. And Davie finally sleeps.

A floor below, a small digital clock on the night table reads 3:30 a.m. Papers lie in sorted piles on a rolltop desk; a cell phone charges. John Wyatt, Davie's grandpa, sleeps in warm flannel pajamas. A geologist engaged in daily battles against assaults on the earth, he is only temporarily worn out. An early riser and ardent networker, he was in bed by nine o'clock and asleep by ten. Last night's town meeting may have been exhausting, but the large turnout was exhilarating. And he had made it happen. Made it uncomfortably clear. The sand rush is on, all right. Nobody is safe. A mining company wants to drill in the Whittakers' backyard over at Green Lake. Grandpa snores softly as his cockatoo, Sierra, dozes in her large covered birdcage.

Outside, high on the bluffs of Baraboo, the earth exhales and sees its bitter cold breath settle as frost. The watchful moon, almost full, awaits the solstice, whispering the language of the ancient tides, of the vast ocean that once covered this rugged terrain a billion years ago. The vast ocean. The massive glacier. A keeper of records, the moon remembers each transformation. As the night ticks along, the lunar glow is paled by a flashback, a vivid memory. The diary of the moon opens.

Long ago, quartzite sand was deposited on top of granite. Great amounts of sand. So much sand, in fact, that stretching to the western border, a sandbox, unrivaled in size, was created. This night, the moon grieves for its treasure as charcoal clouds move in to hide its face. The earth, too, grieves for its sand. Hundreds of millions of years to make grains of pure round quartzite; a few short years for man to remove them—to take them without asking.

The sand. The gift of sand. The curse of sand.

Tonight, there is much uneasiness in the underground world, where a vast dynasty resides. Here the badgers rule. It is a complex kingdom over which they preside. With steadfast determination, they labor as miners of the earth. Mostly unseen, these tireless Mustelids work the bluffs, prairies, and meadows. Like their cousins, the mink, the weasel, and the otter, they burrow for earthworms. They can tunnel for miles, build intricate networks. These sheltered, well-organized apartments have a variety of entrances, bedrooms, toilets, and nurseries. These setts, as they are called, hold the future. Here badger cubs are born and nurtured. And not surprisingly, badgers have few challengers and fewer predators; only the foolish disturb them.

Above and below the surface, animals of every size fear for their survival. There is a great uneasiness, and for good reason; many take their cues from the badgers. Habitat is the key, and very quickly, it is shrinking. There is a blight on the land: frac sand mining.

Ugly open-pit mining is overtaking the landscape, scarring farmland and infiltrating wetland barriers by riverbanks. Even more destructive, complete hilltop removal is taking place. Breathtaking beauty—simply gone. All for sand. The gift of sand. The curse of sand.

The Wisconsin, Baraboo, and Mississippi Rivers wind around tidy and productive dairy farms; but that is changing. The earth, shamelessly defaced, calls for help. Not only by mines, but also in fields and backyards, pyramids of sand rise daily. However, this is no ordinary beach sand; frac sand has a unique shape that makes it useful for energy companies. The quartzite sand itself is just a means to an end, the opening act for fracking. This mining process extracts natural gas and oil from shale rock. But there's a price. Fracking requires drilling wells that *each* use three million pounds of sand. Now there are hundreds of these wells across the country. Feeding the whole process, more than a hundred sand-mining sites scar the face of the Badger State. Big Gas, Big Oil—they have an insatiable hunger for sand. It is an endless cycle as money goes from sand to hand.

There are innocent refugees. Displaced animals panic as fertile pastures become drilling sites. Crisscrossing a field, a desperate badger cannot find the entrance to its sett. A giant pyramid of sand covers the badger's home. In the nursery, young cubs wait for food that never comes. The sett finally collapses as drilling continues. Across the meadow, by a quiet riverbank, an industrious beaver works for months building a dam and a lodge. To feed its young the adept swimmer dives underwater to the lodge's hidden doorway. Frantically, the beaver searches. There is a strange taste and smell to the water. The lodge and all the pups—gone.

There is history here; there are artifacts—evidence of life once lived. At Devil's Lake, by Tumbled Rock Trail, two badgers stop and instinctively listen. For them, the reliable moon tells time. Clues abound in the earth and the December sky. The shortest day is coming—and with it, trouble. A sensitive nose quivers. Every sniff a careful detection, an encrypted message and a code broken. Emerging from the sett, white stripes of a badger face appear like lines on Tunnel Road. A short, wedge-shaped body with a fierce, determined spirit ambles through the brush. Another follows close behind. Like Hermina, their revered ancestor, they have powers. Her future is their present. They sense. They feel. They know.

In a few short days, Earth's retribution for its stolen sand will come. The eve of the winter solstice approaches, and with it, the fifteenth birthday of a young man. When the sun stops and changes its path, he will lead with stone and shield. He will lead with powers of the earth and sky. For on that day, a dark force will emerge from Devil's Lake. Signs are abundant. The drooping hemlock trees mumble through their hanging beards and evergreen boughs. Subtle sounds of warning are replaced by the unearthly noise of machines. Underground quakes cause a chaotic shifting of earth. Purposefully, the badgers hurry onward, driven by the upheaval of their known world.

According to their calculations, the changes began sixty moons ago. Five Winter Hexagons have come and gone since the strangeness began. And each nocturnal vigil brings more questions. Even the mightiest glacier dared not crush or dominate the bluffs of Baraboo. They stand as a symbol of defiance—a totem that rises just north of Devil's Lake. Twelve thousand years ago, these stubborn bluffs forced an unstoppable ice mass—the Wisconsin Glacier—to change its course. These bluffs have stood their ground, and now they must remain intact. Hermina's ancient trust dictates it; integrity requires it.

The badgers head northward where the ancient Baraboo River ripples and winds with age. They lumber over natural rock gardens and root clusters, in search of assistance. From a rocky outcropping, they look to Auriga, the charioteer, the mythic warrior, for the guidance they seek. Quite ironically, their mission will require the committed help of human beings—one for each of the stones. Four special people.

The badgers see these four unique faces as they gaze upward. The constellation speaks silently of the four chosen young warriors: two young men and two young women. There will be Sharon, born of the summer solstice; Carl, born of the autumnal equinox; Melissa, born of the vernal equinox; and Davie, their leader, born of the winter solstice. Each of these chosen warriors, all fifteen years old, will soon receive the gift of Hermina's magical stones. Musta luminae they will be called, once placed in the destined hands. The badgers pause. The delivery of the stones from the lake bottom has been nothing less than dramatic. Joining the badgers for the approaching solstice, friends of scales and of feathers have come forward to help. Just this morning, the musta luminae were found and recovered from the sandy bottom of Devil's Lake. Four walleye—shining, elegant fish—endangered their lives to bring the glistening stones onto the shore. Though camouflaged in a heap of pebbles and small stones, four large ravens picked them up and delivered them. Beneath the sheltering branches of a huge hemlock tree, the badgers retrieved them. Deep in the sett, the stones are now safely guarded. Together the badgers send a cosmic message of thanks to their animal allies.

A sound. Reacting, the larger badger bares razor-sharp teeth and extends fearsome claws. The smaller female, with bristles of silver highlighting her dark coat, moves closer. A piercing wind invades the rocky hollows. As frigid air pummels a giant fir, the great conifer lifts its curved branches in defiance. In the distance, blinding lights emerge and move closer. The high beams reflect upon the sleek black ice on the road. Two, then two more. Two more. A bevy of golden halogen eyes snake around a curve. A caravan of wheels bruises the rounded shoulder of the hill. Close. Closer. A muffled roar rudely replaces the music of the woodland night. Of nocturnal life. The badgers growl a throaty warning. A snowy owl shrieks an answer. A coyote, finding shelter in a badger tunnel, howls support. Like a stalking predator, the caravan moves on and disappears. Finally there is quiet. The startled moon fades from sand to white.

The badgers continue on. Another ridge. Another. Finally they reach a rocky crest. The ancient Baraboo River tumbles below from west to east, with the Baraboo Rapids dancing directly below. Unobstructed, the comfort of the familiar starry dome greets them. Soundless illumination. Clear. Undeniable.

It is time. The summons has come. It is time to pass it on.

The Winter Hexagon
(created with Stellarium)

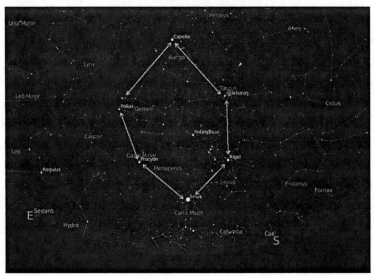

DAVIE

It's crazy early when I awake. And for a change, rock music isn't blaring from my alarm clock, jolting me awake like a Taser. My room, my private observatory, is comforting. On my door there's a sign: "Davie's Crypt." My buddy Carl's idea. He says it's always nighttime in here. He's right. It's perfectly opaque and silent. A kind of paradise. And to add to the paradise factor, now I'm totally free. Yeah. Winter break is here, and it's a beautiful thing. No seven-thirty Spanish class with Mrs. Azzario. That in itself is a huge relief. Math and science, no problem; but my language skills, well, they're kind of nonexistent—like the presence of light inside my room. Since morning is hours away, I can lie still and stare at nothing—just drink in the total blackness of my room. No demands here. No homework. No tests. No pretests or retests. The entire universe is off-limits as I bask in my personal inky black hole.

My walls and ceiling, of course, are black. And no, my parents did not have a fit about the paint job, not at all. They're not, to put it mildly, easily impressed. But when I painted scaled and accurate constellations on my ceiling, they actually took notice. To be honest, I impressed myself with my over-the-top cleverness in using a luminescent white paint from the garage. It was left over after a drive-by handyman painted our house number on the curb last fall.

Oh, I should clarify. I come by my eccentricities honestly. Genetically. My parents, Professor Wyatt and Professor Wyatt, are these world-renowned astronomers. It's a highly contagious profession when it comes

1

down to it. Telescopes and stars tend to be highly addictive. Especially when you get to see the moon through a lens at age three. Really, it if wasn't for daytime stuff like cycling, snowboarding, and skiing, I'd go nocturnal—work at an observatory all night long. Just one small reality check on that: right now, I'm a freshman in high school. But hey, I keep my goal in sight. After all, tomorrow's my birthday and I turn fifteen.

The almanac, according to my grandpa John, another Professor Wyatt, predicts that this year I could be moody, defiant, and a general pain in the butt. Problem is—my parents aren't around enough to make that possible. They have speaking engagements all over the world. They travel constantly. So for me, the classic rebellion routine is pretty limited. The windows of opportunity to enrage them are few. I did get to go with them last summer to New Zealand, possibly the coolest place on planet Earth. Got their attention briefly in my attempt to follow a wombat. Disappeared for half a day. Loved the kookaburras and the koalas. And it was entirely awesome being off my parents' radar. But on Earth, even exotic places are kind of limited compared to what I observe through my telescope. Okay, so there's nothing out there furry and adorable. But galaxy hopping, visiting the great nebula in Orion, heading far beyond the Milky Way—let's be real; that's traveling.

Right now my eyes are aching from overuse. They're probably as red as Mars, as dry as Jupiter. I stayed up almost all night checking out the constellations of the Winter Hexagon. Talk about drama. The myths about the stars are intense. Take the story of Auriga, the charioteer of the sky. That's one of my favorites. It tells about a wounded warrior who won't give up, so he builds a chariot to take him across the sky. Makes me think of my older brother, Richie. He made it back from the war in Iraq minus his left leg and now works at the VA as a physical therapist. He says there are plenty of soldiers who have it a lot worse. That's Auriga for you. One tough piece of star.

Tonight I forced myself to stay up because I had to check out the moon. Tomorrow marks the winter solstice, the shortest day of the year. Before I dozed off, the full moon filled the sky like a mime in whiteface makeup. Large and ghostly. Now, having gotten maybe an hour of sleep, the sane part of me wants to pull the comforter over my head. Instead I flick on the small nightlight. Here it is. My new Celestron SkyProdigy 130 computerized Newtonian auto-alignment telescope. Already I feel a smile breaking through. I can't help it. An undeniable guilt-gift, that's a given. But anyone would pull an all-nighter for this beauty. The big silver bow is still attached to the high-tech altazimuth mount. It's almost an acceptable replacement for my absentee parents, Harriet and George. You never know; although they're in Sydney, Australia, I may be able to get them into focus with this awesome lens.

Not to worry. I'm not entirely an orphan. Thankfully, my dad's dad lives with us. Grandpa is a retired geology professor, a loyal Badger from the U of W, the University of Wisconsin. We connect. Hiking, fishing, and camping, we spend a lot of time together. In many ways, he's actually raising me. He's a real scholar, for sure, but he wears jeans and speaks in reasonably short sentences. If I have anything less than an A on a report card, he doesn't hold it a safe distance away like it's radioactive. Like him, I have fun solving problems, such as we did last weekend when we set up a rain barrel to collect melting snow from the roof. This will provide water for the birdbaths adjacent to each of twelve birdhouses Grandpa has designed as a hobby. Each one is totally different. There's a log cabin, a Zen retreat, a fairy castle—to name a few. In the spring he'll sell them and donate the profits to a wildlife fund.

Now Grandpa may be hard of hearing, but he's cool about it; he sports bright blue hearing aids and owns Bluetooth wireless headphones. He likes Adele and Coldplay. And, by contrast to Harriet and George, he's practical, enjoys fishing, and can fix anything. Even breakfast. I admire that in a scientist. Don't get me wrong; my folks are well-meaning and kind of charming in a geeky kind of way. Speaking of which, there's a borderline embarrassing note attached to the telescope below the ribbon.

Dear Davie,

Happy birthday! Enjoy the Celestron! Know that we love you very much. Unfortunately, the observatory needs our appearance and lecture for their holiday fundraiser. So many budget cuts this year. We'll miss you but expect you'll have a terrific ice-fishing trip with Grandpa. It'll take his mind off the dreadful sand-mining problem for a little while at least. Hugs to your cousins and to Carl. PS: Please no snowboarding on Mrs. Carter's property. Remember what happened last year.

Love, Mom and Dad

Oh yeah, that. Mrs. Carter. In March, snowboarding, I pretty much took out her storage shed. It was kind of shaky to begin with. Hit a brutal patch of ice on the ridge of two crazy-perfect hills. They run parallel, created by some higher power for snowboarders. Great for 180s and other tricks. Anyway, I picked myself up amid crushed and broken plywood without injury—to myself, that is. Yeah, sometimes it happens. You crash and burn. Of course, Grandpa and I rebuilt the shed. Luckily Mrs. Carter stills smiles and waves at me.

Speaking of crash and burn, judging by the flash of light through my window, I'd say a small meteor just landed on the lawn. Something has tripped the outside sensor lights; they're on full blast. It's steady daylight out there. Honestly, I feel invaded, jolted like a mole at sunrise. Something's up. I peer out. Nothing unusual—until I look down. I jump back, startled. Rewind. Double-take. Major *no way*. I have visitors.

On the ground directly below, two midsize chunky animals show their faces. Their black-and-white-striped masks stare up at me. Even from the second floor, I can make out their small, comical ears. Thanks to Grandpa, I know my badgers. These two have the typical wide bodies, wedge-shaped and low to the ground. They have thick necks like those of wrestlers. In a funny kind of way, they remind me of furry hamburgers on wheels. They wobble more than waddle. Amble more than accelerate. Then too, from up here, they look like silver Lotus sports cars with racing stripes. Badgers for sure. Unlike minks, they're one lucky part of the Mustelid family that isn't bred to make fur coats. Thankfully, it's now illegal to hunt them in Wisconsin.

I triple-check. Yeah, they're real all right. But I haven't a clue what on earth these badgers are doing. Here, I mean. Wildlife newsflash:

they're notoriously shy of humans. I'm puzzled. They're waiting—looks like—*patiently*. Hardworking and nocturnal, they should be hunting for food. This is dinnertime. It's weird, so totally out of character. There isn't a lazy bone in a badger body. Grandpa calls them the blue-collar night shift. Says they can dig through asphalt. Tunnel for miles. Bottom line, badgers want to be left alone to forage for food and work construction.

I squint and press my nose up against the glass. Sure enough, the strange couple appears to be searching. Their small, dark eyes lock onto mine, emitting beams of green light right through the glass. For a moment, I'm frozen. I feel my eyes widen. My pupils must be pinpoints. But try as I might, I cannot blink. My eyelids simply will not close, as if a powerful force is holding them open. Before my eyes, colors of every kind appear in tiny squares like digital errors on a television screen. The colors are scrambling. Geometric shapes appear. Circles, ovals, triangles. As in a kaleidoscope, patterns morph from one to another. Finally, images flash and disappear: Jagged cliffs. A giant archway. A portal. I wonder if the badgers are sending a message, a call for help. Somehow, I feel their minds are reaching out to me. The connection is strangely powerful.

Suddenly I'm released. Free to blink. To rub my eyes. The green light is gone. The two badgers remain. I flip the lock and push up the double hung window a few inches. I hear their voices. No words, thank goodness. No words. Instead the badgers start to make sounds—a remarkable orchestra of expressive noises. First a purr. Then a chitter. A pleading whine follows, a low growl, a staccato bark. But I'm not prepared for what follows: a scream—a painful scream of distress almost human in pitch. My chest aches. I feel it. I feel their hurt. I do.

I'm freaked. I break loose and run out of the bedroom. On instinct, I stumble into the dark bathroom and crouch by the narrow window. I can't believe I'm hiding. Or maybe spying. My breath fogs the pane. *Darn these old windows.* The metal lock jabs me in the face as I reposition. Warily, I look out—only to draw my head back like a startled terrier. The badgers know exactly where I am. Together they adjust their heads toward me, looking like a security camera.

My heart pounding, I run barefoot down the hall, stubbing my toe on the metal doorstop. I hop in pain but try not to awaken Grandpa.

His room is directly under mine. I limp back to my bedroom window. Instinctively the badgers redirect their heads in my direction. Somehow I manage to pull on some socks from the many littering my carpet. They're mismatched and inside out. *Insignificant.* I grope for my slippers, my sneakers, anything. I grab a golf club leaning in the corner and sweep it one-handed under the bed. I retrieve ancient Spider-Man slippers covered in dust bunnies. Way too small. A second swipe uncovers my hiking boots, which I pull on untied, laces hanging. When I rub the foggy glass, instead of cold I feel a warm sensation in the palm of my hand. I rub it. Hold my fingers on it. I have no idea where this heat is coming from. Utterly confused, I feel my forehead which, hello, is cool. Now I feel pretty stupid, so I throw up my hands.

The momentum is a bummer. Accidentally, my ring smacks the pane really hard. I watch as the badgers dash for the woods. I suppose something else may have frightened them, but right now, I'll assume the wild look on my face makes me the prime candidate. *I scared them away. Damn.* All I know is that I feel an unexplainable sense of loss; a powerful disappointment. All I manage to do, though, is stand here panting, collecting my thoughts. Then, *zoom.* In the hope the badgers didn't go far, I race like a madman down the stairs. With a turn of the lock, I catapult straight out the mudroom door.

I head to the backyard. Careful to avoid their sharp-pointed spines, I search along the dense hawthorn bushes. A potential hiding place catches my eye. I drop to all fours as the sensor lights suddenly flick off. So much for timing. I rise to my feet in the frustrating darkness. To reactivate the sensor, I flail my arms like a crazed monkey. It works. Beams of light allow me to scan the tough groundcover of low-lying juniper. These gnarly things are ankle-breakers. I avoid stepping in. Instead I reach forward and lift a spindly patch that snaps back with a vengeance, daring me to look further. I don't bother.

Rather, with intense curiosity, I edge around beneath my window. There it is, five yards ahead: the circle of glimmering ice. I pause. Badger tracks are everywhere. Their unmistakable paw prints lead to and from the woods. Wondering if they're watching me, I close my eyes and wait. Strange—the tingling sensation in my palm is increasing from warm to hot. Yet, at the same time, I feel myself shivering almost uncontrollably. My earlobes are freezing. I listen but hear nothing. Then, as my palm begins to burn, I open my eyes and walk forward. Clutching and opening my hand repeatedly makes no difference. The feeling, though uncomfortable, is bearable. I hold my palm up to my face. Touch it with my fingers. The skin is tender, and I can barely discern the outline of a bruise. Forget it. I have no time for it now. The circle of ice, roughly four feet in diameter, captures my focus. Intrigued by what looks like writing, I move closer and forget my burning palm. The badgers have my full attention. I'm awed by what they've left behind.

Carved in the circle is a design both strange and familiar: a spiral. My eyes study the shape, follow its motion. Compelled, I kneel and press my palm down on the ice. Instantly, I feel relief. Then, ever so slowly, I trace the coiled shape while soothing ice crystals melt against my hand. I marvel at this bizarre calling card, this engraving apparently carved by badger claws. As hypnotic as the entrance to a labyrinth, this spiral lures me. It beckons me—summons me like the invisible, the inevitable, pull of the moon.

2

SPIRAL OF STONES

My hand rests at the end of the spiral on four unusual green stones. Like gems, they sit in the very center, commanding attention. Reflecting light. Snow light. Moonlight. Tiny dancing particles glimmer inside them. It's an effort, but I look away, half expecting to see my buddy Carl dive into the woods, enjoying one of his practical jokes. I wouldn't put it past him to be pulling a little stunt with my cousins, Sharon and Melissa. Alone they're okay, but together they're a bunch of pranksters. Why not? We're all spending my birthday weekend together. This would sure get things rolling.

This hunch is short-lived. It vanishes when I pick up the stones. I examine them, roll them around in my hands. But when I hold them in my palm, *the* palm, I can't let go—not because they're pretty or fascinating, which they are, but because I simply cannot toss them to the ground. Not by shaking. Not by flicking. They are now part of my anatomy. A weird kind of force is holding them in place. I'm about to hyperventilate when they drop to the ground. At first I'm relieved. But then I reconsider and scoop them into the wide pocket of my sweatshirt.

I'm cold. My teeth are chattering like the knife of a master chef chopping onions. At this point, I'm thinking hypothermia. Maybe frostbite. Holding my pocket shut and galloping in untied boots is not the way I want to be remembered. So, without any further badger sighting, I reluctantly retrace my steps to the mudroom door. Clambering inside, I close the door abruptly, firmly, and lean my back against it. I don't move until the timer on the outside lights turns off. I sink onto the mudroom bench, take my first deep breath, and kick off my boots. My head rests comfortably against the wall. I'm parched. My throat feels as though I've swallowed the driest continent on the planet, Antarctica. I stand and wobble into the kitchen. The darkness and quiet are comforting. I move toward the soft, familiar humming.

Awkwardly, I open the refrigerator with half-frozen hands and guzzle milk from the half-gallon container. My brain spins as I stare into the fridge in a sleep-deprived, postadrenaline daze. It's either too early for breakfast or I'm too agitated to be hungry. After fishing about, I pull up an uncomfortable wooden chair and bask in the light of the appliance bulb. Nothing on any of the shelves appeals to me. I study the ketchup, the salad dressings on the door, the pickle chips, and several half-full jars of grape jelly. The collection of mustards cracks me up and calms me down. Yellow, brown, deli, Dijon, Dijon with white wine, stone-ground. I try to ignore the brown eggs in sane little compartments on the door of the fridge. Right now, I kind of envy those eggs.

I open the freezer and consider the waffles. Organic blueberry. I move to the toaster, pop in the waffles, and wait, reassuring myself with thoughts of my Saturday-morning routine. In a few short hours, I'll be volunteering at our local animal shelter, the Paw-Paw Patch, where Carl and my cousins join me every week. Founded by a wealthy senior, our nonprofit cares for domestic animals—mostly cats and dogs—until we can finalize adoptions to good homes. We make arrangements for animals to board in temporary foster homes as well. I picture Bear, the Jack Russell terrier who will soon be mine, and the pretty little mutt, Darla, his sidekick and shadow. In ten days, they'll be all healed up and ready to come home with me. This morning there will be plenty to focus on. Especially on busy Saturdays, the regular chores keep me moving until lunchtime.

I need to clear my head, maybe take a short nap till it's time to go. The toaster pops, and a sweet buttery aroma fills the room. I reach for the waffles. That's when I see it—the mark that changes everything. While my eyes stay glued to my hand, I drop the waffles and flick on the over-the-counter light. Smack in the center of my palm is something blue-green, like a tattoo. With just a touch I can tell it's not a bruise. It's a symbol. The all-too-familiar shape appears similar to a human hand. But five curved claws give it away: a badger paw print. I stare at it for a long, long minute. Then, rushing to the sink, I turn on the water, grab a sponge, and rub. I use soap. An abrasive pot scrubber lying in a dish. I scrub hard. Harder. No change. It's there. My head begins to pound. I try not to panic. I mean, it doesn't hurt. But—a major but—this thing, this mark looks convincingly permanent. How am I ever going to explain this? Why me? I'm just a second-generation astronomy geekmeister who loves animals. I'm just Davie.

Forget the waffles; I'm having a hard time swallowing my spit. The mark, I'll admit, is impressive. Striking. Alarming. Exciting. Like a toboggan ride, this bizarre night has me locked in, careening in and out of control, whirling in giant spirals to who knows where.

3

THE MARK

My room is a mess. I'm not sure how I manage it, but when I glance in the mirror, I'm dressed in jeans, a flannel shirt, a zippered sweatshirt, and a down vest. I ignore my right hand. At least I can picture the day shaping up. Saturday morning at the Paw-Paw Patch. Always fun. Plenty of time outside. Because it's less than a week until Christmas, there will be a lot of animal adoptions today. Pets, unfortunately, don't always make good holiday gifts. It's important to be prepared and ready for an animal. Usually, after the New Year, we have some returns. It's sad. When that happens, we all try to give the dog or cat some extra love. Sharon gets on the phone and networks. She's very detail oriented and informative. She gets to the point, handles paperwork for Mrs. Peterson, and speeds up the adoption process. Most questions go to Sharon. Melissa gets animals ready and out the door in a different way. She can be very charming and funny. She likes to talk animal personalities. In fact, she always manages to highlight their best, most adorable qualities. Leave it to Melissa to primp a pit bull, make quirks sound like talents. With her collection of donated accessories, she's always there for the ones that need pizzazz. Carl likes to handle the heavy stuff, such as the forty-pound bags of dry dog food. He has a macho thing going, which is fine with me. Weight-wise, he's 160 to my 130. The hand truck works for me.

I picture my two favorite dogs eating happily from bowls in the warm kitchen. I've kept my eyes on them for six weeks while they've been treated for minor injuries. Bear, who runs like a streak of white lightning, is recovering from a bad ear infection that keeps one ear sticking sideways like a bat's. The enthusiastic little guy is always wide open. He's also an escape artist, which is how he wound up here in the first place. Except for two brown patches, one around his left eye and a big heart shape on his back, he's solid white when not rolling in puddles. Then there's sweet Darla, with springs for legs. Part dachshund, part Chihuahua, Melissa calls her a "doxie-wawa." Rescued from a hoarding situation, her five puppies were quickly adopted out to good homes. Ten pounds and 100 percent love, Darla adores Bear. He tolerates her and protects her. I figure they make a good brother–little sister package. I've filled out the paperwork. Grandpa cosigned. Harriet and George kind of agreed in theory. Both dogs will be mine December 31. I already have outings planned for them. We'll walk and hike every day. Keep each other in super shape. That's the plan.

Yet now, even with so much to look forward to, my thoughts return to the badgers and the green stones. To the pocket of my sweatshirt. To my hand. Urgently, I head over to my dresser and grab a pair of fingerless black wool gloves I use for chores around the shelter. They cover the mark completely. Instantly, I feel calmer. Yeah, I'm good. Less distracted. I picture skiing on the Ice Age Trail. A whole afternoon of cross-country. The snow on the trail perfect. After we finish around eleven, the four of us will head out together. I'm suddenly very hungry.

Heading toward the kitchen, I smell oatmeal. Grandpa must be up and dressed. I enter just as he opens the outside door to check the thermometer. With his thick white curly hair and large gray eyes, he looks like a snowy owl. He turns around and brushes a few ice crystals from his hair.

"Well, Davie!" He looks surprised to see me up. "It's a whopping ten degrees out there!"

"Hopefully it'll warm up to like, fifteen, by this afternoon."

He laughs. "Tell me—what d'ya have goin' on?" He moves around the kitchen with his usual early-morning high energy.

"The shelter. Then cross-country with Carl, Melissa, and Sharon."

"Well, you'll be fine while you're movin' steady; that's for sure." He taps his hand on the counter while he watches the coffeemaker. "Got some Road Rage brewin'. Want some?"

"Yeah, sure. I could use some coffee." The dinger goes off. Grandpa rubs his hands together and grabs two mugs.

"Forecastin' the same for tomorrow. Course, that'll be perfect weather for ice fishin' if the sun stays out. Otherwise, checkin' those tip-ups out on the ice will be tough. Yep, if we're lucky, the wind won't be blowin' off the cranberry bogs!"

The annual ice-fishing trip is something special—a sacred ritual kind of thing.

Grandpa hands me a mug. It's half full. I stare into a cup of steaming blackness and fill the rest up with milk. In five minutes, I hear the sound of an engine outside.

"Grandpa, gotta go! Carl and his dad are here. I'll see you later!"

I rip my ski jacket from the hook. Instantly I change my mind and reach for my warm but lighter-weight jacket. Cross-country is a tough workout, and it's best not too overdress. I fill a wide mug to the top with hot oatmeal and take a plastic spoon from the drawer. By the door, I grab my tall, lightweight skis. It must be seven sharp; that's when the Marcials, Carl and his dad, arrive every Saturday in their sturdy navy-blue station wagon. It's an old Volvo that Carl calls "the shoebox on wheels." But hey—it works. And it has an amazing roof rack for anything and everything we can't fit inside. Carl jumps out and stashes my skis on top. I pull on my orange fleece ski hat.

"No hat, Carl? Guess you don't want to mess your hair for Melissa." I don't blame him. Carl's hair is a thick mass of shiny black curls. This is true lady-killer hair. Next to him, my hair looks like a neglected hanging plant. Naturally, I know for a fact that my best friend is taken with my gorgeous cousin. I guess it makes sense. She's a knockout, and he's all the things girls like. Though Carl is shorter than me, his build is muscular, thick and rugged. But he's cool. Like, he doesn't know how handsome he is. Next to him, I'm three inches taller and lean. I mean, I'm in good shape. Really fit. Tough like a hockey stick. Problem is, I keep growing longer—like maybe an inch a month. No matter how much I eat, I can't seem to bulk up.

"Ola, Davie!" Mr. Marcial calls over his shoulder. He manages the Paw-Paw Patch, which has a waiting list for volunteers. Why? Because he's outgoing and kind. He's known fondly as *St. Francis* by Mrs. Peterson, the receptionist.

"Morning, Mr. Marcial." My face feels flushed and I'm heating up like a furnace. I remove my hat. But that's when I realize the heat is coming from my right hand. It's pulsing.

"Would it be okay to turn down the heat?"

"No problem," answers Mr. Marcial. "I was just trying to thaw my Peruvian genes, that's all. You'd think after all these years I'd get used to the winter here. But this isn't just cold—it's liquid nitrogen. Wisconsin cold!" He laughs a hearty laugh.

"Yeah," says Carl, "it's a good thing we found Blackie and took him inside. Snakes can't deal with this weather."

"Uh ... speaking of which ... you fellas better make sure Blackie is in his cage when you leave today. There have been sightings, shall we say, at the front desk."

"Oh, that," replies Carl, throwing me a guilty look. "Blackie just needed a little change of scenery. Besides, king snakes need room. He was too cramped in his cage, Dad."

"Well, all five feet of him was spotted by Mrs. Peterson. She said she was caught 'off guard' while closing up. I'd say she was being diplomatic."

"Sorry, Dad."

Mr. Marcial flashes a quick wrinkled-brow glance at Carl. "We've talked too many times about practical jokes." He glances in the rearview mirror. "My son likes to get my goat." Carl slumps lower in his seat but winks back at me.

"Everyone in the shelter knows Blackie is harmless, Dad."

"Everyone except Mrs. Peterson, it seems. Enough said."

"Okay, okay."

After several winding turns, we drive up to the entrance of the Paw-Paw Patch. Luckily for me and Carl, several volunteers have just finished shoveling the driveway.

"I'd call that good timing!" Carl says as he opens the car door.

"Oh, don't worry," answers his dad. "You'll have plenty of kitty litter to shovel."

I jump out. The shelter is a sprawling wooden farmhouse that's been enlarged year after year. Fifteen acres and the sprawling two-story house were donated by a generous animal-loving senior. That was roughly ten years ago. White paint has peeled from the trim, and a few roof shingles are missing here and there. But overall, the layout works great since there are a lot of small rooms. That's how we separate the domestic pets from the varied wildlife creatures that show up. There are snakes, an occasional horse, a rare barn owl. Right now we have a badger cub who curls up in a small doggie bed. Amazingly cute. Follows us around like a puppy when out of the cage. A telephone lineman found the cub alone by the side of the road. He waited. No adult badgers showed up. Of course, after Easter, there's always an array of bunnies and chicks. This makes Mr. Marcial talk angrily in Spanish. Unlike Carl, I don't speak Spanish, but the meaning is clear: animals are not toys.

Off to the left, a now empty carport houses litters of puppies that nurse and play in the early summer. In the back is a large run for the dogs, designed as a kind of bark park with double doors for extra security. Except for the exceptional digger or jumper, it's pretty much escape proof. Most often, our four-legged escapees return around dinnertime. Farthest back, beyond the run, there's a lovely pasture edged with shade trees. During the winter, barn animals are kept in the small stable that used to be a carriage house. At the moment, we have only one horse, an Appaloosa, and one restless ram.

After stomping the snow from our boots on a wiry cat mat, Carl and I enter to the familiar welcoming sounds—hellos of every kind and every pitch: barks, growls, howls, meows, hisses, caws, and screeches. Yeah, there's no sneaking around here. All the noses, muzzles, snouts, and beaks are sniffing things out 24-7. It would take a Dr. Dolittle to translate all the animal gossip, comments, and complaints. Naturally, I try my best to keep the peace. From working here, I've gotten really good at reading animals. If there's tension, I separate them. Because dogs evolved from wolves, alpha leaders are best kept apart. Come to think of it, that might be true of humans too.

We throw off our jackets and head toward the large bags of dry food. This is the grunt work: feeding the animals, filling water bowls, cleaning cages and crates with a mixture of Clorox and water. There's a separate crew that takes care of the stalls out back, places fresh hay, exercises the larger animals. Anxious to get started on baths, I walk over to a cage with a green slip attached to the latch. This means, Izzy, a medium-sized mutt, has been adopted. His side is shaved in a circular patch where stitches have healed from a wound. He sees me, and his stubby tail goes wild. Honestly, he has to be the homeliest dog I have ever seen, and probably one of the sweetest. His long, rough coat, badly in need of a trim, is gray. His hopeful brown eyes are set unusually wide apart for his face. The tip of one ear is missing, and he has an overbite.

"Izzy boy, you're gonna have a real home tomorrow." I lift him up and hold thirty pounds of licking maniac. He's glad to see me. I scratch under his chin and let him hang over my shoulder for a bit. I'm excited for Izzy. "How about an express wash?" I grab a washcloth and a doggie toy. By now I'm used to his toothy smile. "If I were you, Izzy, I'd keep my mouth closed for pictures, okay?"

"Hey, where are the girls?" Carl asks. "They're late."

I glance at my watch. "They should be here pretty soon. Sharon's gonna help me with the baths. And, well, you know Melissa. At this point—"

"Strictly fashion show," Carl says, finishing my thought. He opens a giant carton of donated dog shampoo and hands me a bottle. "Here. Honey oatmeal."

Ten days away, the annual New Year's Pet Fashion Show is the biggest moneymaker of the year. There are a dozen or more local sponsors, and the shelter is always jam packed. The mayor of Baraboo usually attends with members of the city council. Local radio and television celebrities help with publicity.

"Hey, not to worry, Carlito. Melissa needs a date for the show." Carl's face lights up. He's my best friend and totally awesome, but I can't help but envy that grin of perfect white teeth. They contrast with his clear olive skin. Really. He reminds me of Zorro.

I put Izzy into a tub and in a motion of solidarity touch a zit forming on my forehead. "Here we go, fella." I turn on the spray and use a special leash to hold him in place. He's a good sport. He wags his tail continuously.

Meanwhile, Carl empties the box and places the shampoo bottles in neat rows. The door of the cabinet tilts at a weird angle. He grabs a screwdriver to fix it.

"Don't forget," he reminds me, "we'll have to hide Mr. Tut. He hates wearing clothes." Carl is referring to a Siamese cat, an old gentleman who lives permanently at the Paw-Paw Patch. He's a shelter pet who enjoys a comfortable life in his personal kitty condo.

"Okay, Izzy, hold still." Soap is everywhere. I can't help but crack up at the dog's skinny body beneath all that fur.

"Hey, Carl, remember the March of the Mutts?"

"That was fantastic. Everyone got adopted."

"Who could forget those outfits."

"Tuxedos. Top hats and tails." Carl closes the cabinet, takes the screwdriver and tightens the wobbly door. Satisfied, he tightens the door handle. "Izzy, you are one lucky Mutt. Good luck." One quick pet, and Carl exits to the storage room. I see it in his face, though. It's hard not to get attached.

"Yeah. Just in time to escape doggie auditions today." Finally I turn off the water and dry Izzy in an old towel. He's terrified of hair dryers.

At that very moment, drama enters in the form of Melissa. "Clear the way!" she announces as she carries assorted shopping bags piled high with scarves, fake pearls, hats, and hangers. Behind her, Sharon peers over the large cardboard box she's carrying with a look of exasperation on her face. She crosses her eyes at me. I cross mine back.

I grab a towel. "Look, Izzy, the fashionistas are here."

"Fashionista—*singular*," Sharon corrects. "Would someone save me? My sister is out of her mind. She's been torturing me all week."

"Oh, please!"

"What do you call stringing endless necklaces of fake pearls while I'm trying to watch the skiing competition on TV?"

Melissa tosses her celery-straight shiny hair. "Do you want our animals adopted or not? They have to look their best."

"They look just fine with a nice collar and a little bio."

"You're missing the point! They need to stand out. Catch someone's eye. Make an impression!" Melissa stops, turns in her knee-high suede boots, and glares. She picks her long hair up into a ponytail and drops it back down. "You're just not into it."

"I'm doing my part, but it's never enough." Sharon, all of five feet two, makes her stand. Her green eyes pierce like darts. "That's it, Miss Doggie Dior. I've made my last bow tie!" Sharon drops the box of costumes on the counter, takes Izzy gently from my arms, and carries him off to get settled in his crate. In a minute, she'll be back with another dirty dog for round number two. I watch as Sharon instantly returns with a mutt of epic proportions.

"We'll have to double-team this guy," Sharon says, straining with the leash. Part German shepherd, part Great Dane, with a touch of blue-eyed husky, this dog must weigh more than I do. I can tell by his ears that water is his enemy. I prep for battle by grabbing a sizable dog treat. I suppose, for a lightweight contender, I pull my weight around the Paw-Paw Patch; by the end of the morning, if I don't run out of steam or shampoo, I'll easily have gone ten rounds.

4

ZIGS AND ZAGS

By eleven o'clock, I throw in the towel. Literally. Done with bathtime, I'm the one soaked from head to toe. Sharon isn't much better off. From experience, we both keep an extra set of clothes here for days like this. Morning chores completed, we change clothes and head to the kitchen area. Carl is already removing a pile of sandwiches and chips from a paper bag. His mom always sends a Saturday lunch for all of us. Anxious to get moving, I run down the hall and check on Melissa. Stuck in fashion designer mode, she has to be coaxed away from her squirming, four-legged models. I liberate three Chihuahua sisters from ballerina tutus in different pastel colors. Music from *The Nutcracker* is playing in the background. Melissa drags me to the glass-enclosed display area facing the entrance door. Here are five adorable pit bull puppies all dressed in little orange T-shirts. The mother dog wears a bright orange jailhouse jumpsuit marked "Inmates at Work."

"You know, Melissa, I envy the doggie rejects."

"What are you talking about?"

"The dogs excused from modeling. At least *they're* playing happily in the snow."

"Is that a hint?"

"Yes, it is. Carl's looking for you. Time to go."

"My theme is lost on you, I see."

Equally impatient to get rolling, Sharon stands by the door. She's wearing cross-country shoes that look just like sneakers. While Melissa takes a yogurt from the fridge, Sharon and I step outside. Carl is busy spreading salt on the sidewalk.

"Where's Melissa?"

"Oh, she's coming."

Carl adjusts the flashlight and knife on his belt and checks to make sure his compass is handy. He used to be into scouting and has a ton of badges. Although he abandoned that a while ago, he's always well prepared for whatever. I'm serious. If there's ever any danger, I want Carl by my side. By the way he checks his watch, it's clear he's done waiting. He dashes inside for his lightweight backpack and returns pulling Melissa by the hand. She looks fresh off the runway. Sleek and slender. The white nylon jumpsuit is impractical but a total knockout. *You go, Carl.*

Right now, weather conditions look good. The snow is well-packed, and the sun is shining. From the time we snap into our skis, I figure we'll have roughly four hours of daylight.

"Let's head over to the Baraboo Golf Club," Melissa suggests, adjusting the headband that covers her ears. "We can ski there."

Sharon quickly vetoes that idea. "You're kidding, right? I was hoping we'd ski some of the Devil's Lake Segment."

The choices: easy or hard, one extreme or another. Carl comes up with a good compromise. He suggests a reasonable route from our current location on Matts Ferry Road. We'll head over to Old Lake Road. From there we can head south a few miles toward the northern entrance of Devil's Lake State Park. Of moderate difficulty, this is a connector route of the Ice Age Trail that will do just fine.

"It's a nice straight shot," Carl explains. "Trust me. It's about five or six miles round-trip. We can do that no problem."

It's agreeable. We head out in single file, passing clusters of tall red cedar and thick groves of bare maple. Further on, towering above us, the branches of fir trees drop pellets of snow as we pass. There's a gradual uphill stretch for fifty yards. We stop to catch our breath.

"Cross-country burns more calories than any other sport," announces Melissa. "Really, it's a super fat-burner."

Sharon shakes her head in disbelief. "As if you have any fat to burn. You're a stick." Melissa, several inches taller than Sharon, is ballerina slender. With more than a touch of envy, Sharon blurts out the obvious. "Oh, come on. That white jumpsuit you're wearing would make anyone else look like a puffball. A marshmallow, at least."

"A woman can't be too skinny or too rich."

"Who exactly are you quoting?"

"Anyone who's anyone in the fashion world. All the great designers."

"Looking like a mannequin. That's quite a goal, Missy."

"No, it's about looking fabulous. Having sophistication."

"But that's all just outside." Sharon's expressive eyes are fun to watch, especially when she rolls them. "Clothes and more clothes. Nobody has ever successfully entered your room."

"I do every day."

"There's clothing everywhere. Heaps. No ... dunes. There are two hat racks piled high with hats, scarves, costume jewelry, handbags. And I believe there's a shoe rack hidden somewhere beneath a mountain of sandals, shoes, and boots."

"Unlike you, I don't shop L. L. Bean. You do your thing; I do mine."

To break the tension, I reach in a side pocket and give Melissa the only accessory she'll need on our trip: a reflective orange headband. I'm just trying to be funny. And practical. Instead, I almost get a ski pole through the heart.

"Since you're wearing white, take this just in case we lose you."

"No way, Davie, that's hideous."

"Be warned. It's hunting season." I hide my smile.

"Get out." Melissa shoves me away.

"Don't worry. Nobody's hunting for snowshoe bunnies." She glares at me with amber darts. I shrug. "Just kidding."

"That's hilarious, Davie," Melissa warns, waving her ski pole. "Where do you want me to put this?"

"Enough, guys." Carl intervenes. He gently redirects her poles, placing the straps around her wrists. "Okay. Good to go." Surprisingly, Melissa exchanges headbands.

Sure. It's no wonder Carl's taken by Melissa's force field. Even the orange headband looks awesome on her auburn hair. Carl stays back and skis behind Melissa while I push ahead with Sharon. Though the snow is well-packed, it's stop-and-go until we get to the trailhead. A few large boulders make for sharp turns in an area of dry prairie. There are bare patches where the snow has blown away. And here, like petrified bouquets, I notice the dry remnants of sunflower, goldenrod, and aster. Sharon stops on a crest overlooking a broad downhill stretch. This is what we've come for. Now we make tracks, skiing on for a mile or more before we gather again.

"For those of us who *do* eat normally," she says, "I've got Luna Bars in my backpack."

"Go for it," Melissa snaps. "Extra calories and skinny jeans don't mix."

"Yeah, right."

"Really. Someday I'll be living in New York City, working on Seventh Avenue. I'll have a personal shopper at Saks Fifth Avenue. You'll be welcome to visit me in my duplex."

"Whatever." That said, Sharon hurls herself off the ridge, gets up speed and moguls perfectly over a gnarly tree root. My cousins have been at each other since their dad up and left them and their mom. That was a couple of months ago. Obviously there's a lot of anger flying around. Having provoked her sister, Sharon just keeps going like she's trying to break a record for endurance. Carl may be the Eagle Scout, Melissa the model, but Sharon is the amazing athlete. In competition, Sharon appears fearless. Her focus is intense and complete. When she races, she soars like a peregrine falcon released back into the wild. No joke. She trains really hard. And speaking of rooms, hers is an insane workout zone. She has a treadmill, a recumbent bike, a chin-up bar, and a multitude of free weights in every size and color. Her workout videos are killers. Forget it. I've borrowed a couple.

At last, winter quiet surrounds us and all I can hear is the swoosh of my skis. We reach the blue marker that identifies all connector routes. This is good. We're on the right track. Actually, our journey today is only a freckle on the face of the Ice Age Loop. Twelve hundred miles long, the trail runs all the way through Wisconsin. The Devil's Lake Segment, the Sauk Point Segment, and the Merrimac Segment are nearby, but they're more suitable for hiking—in warmer months.

Suddenly, just beyond the marker, there's movement in the woods.

To my right, I spot a white-tailed deer picking at the remains of bluestem grass, now a coppery red. Ahead, a squirrel scurries up the truck of a tall maple. Afternoon sunlight glimmers on the snow-covered branches like a hundred tiny mirrors. My stride becomes steady and even, almost like a running gait. I use my poles when I need to manage an incline. A fine dusting of powder hits my face. I feel totally delightfully awake. Around a curve, we come upon a sign: "Devil's Lake State Park – 2 miles." Soon the path flattens out and widens so that we can ski side by side. Hardy juniper climbs up the embankments on both sides. Cruising along, I find the dependable gait, the rhythmic motion of skis and poles, hypnotic. Right, left, right, left, each arm in opposition to the forward ski. I feel in sync with myself. It's a good feeling.

But then my balance falters. The terrain becomes rough and uneven. When I squeeze my ski poles, my palm starts to burn uncomfortably. Friction can't be the cause, but I loosen my grip and use my poles only for balance. Determined to make it to the park entrance, I ignore the burn and keep going. Sweet piney air hits my face, reviving me, encouraging me to continue. The scent of evergreen and earth surrounds me as if exhaled by the dense, unspoiled woods. Again I find the steady opposition of arms and legs strenuous but satisfying. The path rises before me. My speed propels me up the snowy incline to another sign: "Devil's Lake State Park."

A cracking noise alerts me. The sound of splitting wood is suddenly followed by a boom. Broom-shaped branches hit and sweep the ground. Completely uprooted, a tall white pine has landed directly in my path. Adrenaline surges through my body. I assemble my skis and grind to a sudden halt. A cascade of snow fills the air along with a barrage of debris. Sharp pieces of bark fly as I shield my face. I struggle to catch a full breath. I'm lucky. Incredibly. The pine tree lies with its enormous root ball less than two yards away.

Sharon races back to me with long, even strides. Melissa and Carl must be pretty far back. They haven't come into view. Sharon stops on a dime, churning up snow like a snowmobile. She chucks her skis, then scrambles around the tree and rushes over to me. Her freckled cheeks are bright red from exertion.

"Davie! What's going on? You okay?"

"I think all body parts are accounted for." My forehead feels slick with perspiration.

Sharon stares. "God, that was close! That tree almost—"

"*Almost* is good." I look around in a daze. Carl catches up and skis over. His wide brown eyes size up the situation and tell me what I won't admit out loud. *I could have been splat.*

"Davie! Jeez! What'd you do to that pine?" Playfully, Carl smacks me with my orange hat, which has fallen in the snow. "Remember the motto—*leave no trace?*"

Sharon shrugs. "Not a scratch on him, Carl. You can put the meds away."

I watch as he puts the first aid kit back in his pouch. Melissa catches up, looking pissed off.

"Anything to be the center of attention, huh?"

"Yeah. Davie ran into a problem," Carl says as he puts his arm around my shoulder. "Guess you'll live to change another cat box, Wyatt!" Then he shoves me into the snow.

We laugh, yet instinctively, something feels very wrong to me. The pine uprooting out of nowhere, my burning hand—these were warnings. I ignored them. Undeniably, this crazy mark, this paw print, functions as a kind of GPS. Or radar. Or sonar. I just don't know yet. I feel alone and confused. My secret is weighing me down. Determined to lighten up, I scoop up a handful of snow. The icy cold feels soothing even through my black gloves. My fingertips, though, are another story. The fat snowball I toss at Carl hits him smack on his broad chest. In a flash, he ducks behind the thick trunk of an oak. My next snowball misses its target. In seconds, I'm hit with a barrage of snowballs coming from all directions. Melissa shrieks.

By the end of the onslaught, the mark has cooled. With one last juicy snowball, I take aim. I target the back of Sharon's snow-crusted jacket as she retreats. She turns and jumps on my back. I spin around until we fall. This totally beats skiing. We goof around until we're all camouflaged in white like Melissa. But somehow even this distraction can't block out invading thoughts of the badgers, the spiral, the green stones. I raise my hand to call a truce. It's time to head back.

26

"Okay, we're moving out! I'll lead off."

We follow a line of slender birch. The trunks look like peeling parchment. A bright red cardinal lands on a curvy branch, a stunning contrast to the snowy background. Along a curve of uphill terrain, the rising steps of a stream create dozens of small frozen waterfalls. The stream zigzags, reminding me of the Baraboo River as it loops horizontally on the map. As the stream widens, icy water gurgles over rocks and rounded stones. Purple stones, pink stones, swirly orange stones. Instantly I feel a pang of guilt. Then a sharper jolt. The green stones! I've been careless with them. They've been in the pocket of my sweatshirt all this time, unsecured. What have I been thinking? If only Carl, Sharon and Melissa knew, then I wouldn't have to deal with this alone. As soon as possible, I have to tell them. The whole thing, the whole story. If not, I'll burst like a pinecone in a forest fire.

The whitening sun seems to reflect on every surface. I make a visor with my right hand. Above, the fir trees dangle diamond earrings. I feel almost dizzy as the sun moves about like a spotlight. The effect is dazzling, disarming, magical. I stop before I stumble in this glistening haze. With hesitation, I reach into my sweatshirt pocket. To my intense relief, the four stones are still there. Quickly, with my back turned, I move them to the zippered inside pocket of my jacket. I breath a huge sigh. I have to protect them. These strange luminous stones are in my care. I turn. Everywhere, magic surrounds me.

5

STRANGE VIBRATIONS

Sharon confides in me.

"Listen, Davie. It's the weirdest thing. Right before that pine came crashing down, I felt something weird. I'm not sure what it was. The ground under me was … well, sort of vibrating. Like a small quake or something."

I think back. All I recall is the burning intensity of the mark. "That giant root ball—that's probably what you felt."

"Yeah, maybe. Maybe."

Further along, I come upon hickory nuts scattered on a thin patch of white snow. A strange sight for late December. I'd expect the wildlife to have carried the nuts away by now. The sun is higher. It's getting warmer. I open my jacket. At a crossroads fifty yards ahead, we all gather by a faded wooden sign. The lettering is partly covered with a thin layer of ice. Sharon and Melissa use their poles to try to scrape it off. Finally Carl uses the handle of his pole to give a firm tap, and the ice falls off in chunks.

Parfrey's Glen>4 miles
<Gall Rd/Steineke Rd>

Carl's eyes brighten at the thought of an exploration. "Parfrey's Glen. Heard of the place, but I've never been."

"Too far," Melissa says.

"Not good skiing terrain either," Sharon adds. "Been there with Grandpa, right Davie?"

"Yeah. Touch with your eyes." The words just pop out of my mouth.

"What?"

"Oh, something Grandpa told me—told us."

Melissa laughs. "He still says it all the time."

Instantly, pictures start to form from a summer trip to the glen. Sharon, Melissa, and I were there as kids with Grandpa John. I recall a narrow gorge at the base, loaded with ferns and moss. I was grumpy because we couldn't bring his big dog, Terrence. I didn't understand. Naturally, Grandpa had to explain what a *protected* area was. I kept asking, "Protected from what?" It was bustling with wildlife, like everywhere. Deer munched on a huge abundance of plants. Grandpa made us promise to remain totally silent. I saw my first beaver in that glen. And when I reached to take a praying mantis from a leaf, Grandpa said those four words.

"Parfrey's Glen is way on the other side of the park," Sharon says. "But there's a pretty trail if we head left. It works its way toward Hill Street."

"The road that crosses the railroad tracks, right?"

"Uh huh."

"That's a nice trail." Carl nods.

"Agreed?"

We stride along until the path gradually narrows. Overgrown blackberry brambles interfere and then block our way. Using our poles, we try to clear the wild tangles. These plants are vicious any time of the year, but it very obvious this trail hasn't been used for quite a while.

I feel it. The mark on my hand starts to burn. I have an urge to turn back to the sign and go right instead of left. But Sharon and Carl seem anxious to trudge ahead. As soon as we manage to cut through, we're tangled again. On either side, overgrown vegetation covers midsize boulders. They remind me of fishing nets as they drape, catching our ankles.

With his knife, Carl detaches a creeper from his leg. "Man, these vines are dense little monsters."

Just slightly ahead, Sharon slashes away like Katniss in the Hunger Games. Excitedly, she calls out and waves her ski poles in the air.

"Hey, guys! Check it out. I found something cool. Looks like the secret garden!"

The hidden metal archway seems out of place and very rusted. In fact, it looks like we might be on somebody's private property—not unusual for certain parts of the Ice Age Trail.

"Let's leave our skis and explore." I'm about to object, but Sharon doesn't wait for an answer. She and Carl release their skis in a flash and leave them standing upright in the snow. I relent and do the same. Melissa stabs her skis with supreme annoyance. Then I rush to follow "Lewis and Clark"—with Melissa objecting behind me.

"Well, just for a very short distance," Melissa says. "I don't want to catch my clothes on these nasty thorns."

"Just stay close behind me."

"I didn't think we'd be roughing it!" she grumbles, grabbing on to the back of my jacket.

The path twists right and left numerous times and then, surprisingly, disappears. I practically knock into Sharon and Carl. They are crouching, looking down. Melissa is on my heels, pushing me forward. "Wish those turkeys would wait up …"

I put my hand out. "Hold on. Stop!"

"So what is the big discovery?"

"Careful, you guys," Sharon warns. "Don't come any further."

Carl stands up but keeps staring at a major drop in the ground. "It looks … it looks like a sinkhole."

"A what?" Melissa asks, peering over my shoulder.

"A sinkhole. Where the earth kind of caves in." I've heard of these but never seen one. There's a gaping hole maybe thirty feet in diameter. No joke. It looks like we're standing at the edge of a moon crater. I've seen plenty of those through my telescope. The hole is full of dirt, rocks, and hard frozen mud.

Melissa grips my arm like a blood pressure cuff. "Oh no! What about where we're standing?"

"Okay," Carl says calmly, "let's everybody back up. Go on!" With

31

Melissa clinging like a barnacle, Carl and Sharon right behind, I retrace the winding path until it straightens out. Then we run like maniacs until we see the archway. I drop my poles. It's a major relief to see our skis standing in the snow, waiting for us like candy canes.

"This is freaky!" Melissa exclaims, hurrying to her skis.

Sharon agrees, meeting my eyes with a huge roll of her own. "So not good."

I defer to Carl. "When do you suppose it happened?"

Carl steps into his skis. "Well, the mud at the bottom is frozen solid. So I doubt it happened today."

I agree with Carl but have more questions. "So why isn't the site closed off?"

"That probably means," Melissa answers, "the park rangers have no idea it's even there."

"Maybe we should call it in right now," Sharon says, turning to Carl.

Carl tries his cell phone. "No service. Let's try a little father north. We can't be too far from the golf course."

"That figures," Melissa reminds us. "My idea in the first place. But no, Sharon needs a challenge. We could well be saying our prayers in a frosty pit right now."

"Now that's an uplifting thought," Sharon replies. "Or we could be circling the ninth hole—how thrilling."

Two crows suddenly take off. They leave their loud caws behind, hanging in the air.

The comparison is hard to resist. "There they go ... Sharon and Melissa!" We make our way steadily along Gall Road.

"Where are all the animals today?" Carl asks. "There's supposed to be this overabundance of wildlife."

"Where'd you hear that?" I ask. "So far today, I can count them on my fingers. Usually we see a lot more white-tailed deer and snowshoe rabbits. We always hear woodpeckers."

Carl shrugs. "Get this—it was one of those boring news magazines. My dad was reading the article. 'Beasts on the Rise' was the title. Showed a deer in a motel room, a wild turkey on someone's deck. A moose foraging around an apartment complex. Pretty sad."

"They shot a bear," I add, "near the Dumpster of a restaurant. Makes me sick."

A bad attempt at humor carries us up the final stretch. Melissa sings "The Bear Went Over the Mountain."

"Cut it out, Melissa," Sharon scolds. "Not funny."

"Sorry. You're right." Melissa tears up. "I ... I just like that old song. That's all."

We fall silent. At this point, there's lots of poling required. With a percussive rhythm in my head, I push forward with the extra effort of nearing a finish line. I lead, and everyone else keeps pace. When we stop briefly, Carl tries his cell phone again, this time successfully. Since Grandpa is cooking, Avery will meet us by the southeast edge of the golf course. Good news. It's not far. But the discovery of the sinkhole—that really has me worried. I've barely noticed; the light is fading fast. There's no room for mistakes. I have to take it slow with extreme focus on the terrain, observant of where I put my skis. Our lives may depend on it.

6

EYES ON THE ROAD

At last, we gather together on a small ridge. The gray zigzags of this main access road are a heck of a welcome sight.

"Civilization!" Melissa announces, raising her ski poles in the air. Her cheeks are pink, her eyes the bright color of amber. "Didn't see my pretty birds today, though. That's disappointing. I missed the pine grosbeaks, all plump and rosy. And the purple finches, looking like they were dipped in cranberry juice. I missed them most of all."

"There were a couple of crows …"

"Shut up, Davie."

"And there was," Carl adds, "a sighting of one woodpecker."

Melissa counters. "That was a telephone lineman in disguise."

"Hey, Carl," Sharon says, "remember that aggressive bird? The blue jay that attacked and stole your whole bag of peanuts?"

"Yeah, He was Special Forces. No doubt. A clean extraction."

"He was bold," I reply. "And crazy. Female birds don't take chances. They dress a lot smarter, more practical. For survival, camouflage works best."

"Welcome to the Birds of a Feather Fashion Show," Melissa announces. "And here, smartly dressed in a cranberry tuxedo, is Mr. Purple Finch. Notice the contrasting gray pants. Next to him, right down the aisle hops Mrs. Finch, dressed in last year's faded housedress."

I can hardly keep a straight face. "Well, out here, one false move and you're dinner."

"Proving, of course," Sharon says, "animals are smarter than we are. While we're getting assaulted by nature—"

"Pelted by ice," Melissa grumbles.

"Threatened by falling trees and sinkholes," I add.

"Proving, of course," Sharon finishes with a knowing tilt of her head, "the animals are dressing in fatigues."

"Or," Carl says, "they're holed up in their cozy dens. Watching cable, no doubt."

Melissa calls out to the silent woods, "I vote for hibernation!"

"Nothing I'd like more." Carl pulls Melissa against him.

"There's your animal!" I gesture toward Carl.

He grins proudly and, without letting go of Melissa, checks his phone for a text from Avery. "Hey, Avery's on his way."

We come to a clearing edged by elm and basswood. At the far corner sits a small wooden cabin. The broken-down structure looks as if it's been unoccupied for decades. The grayish logs have been worn down by harsh weather, and there is mortar missing in places. I notice the roof is missing gutters. The small square front window has two panes of glass where four once were. One of the remaining panes is crisscrossed with cracks, and the other appears to have been shot through with a BB gun. The entire cabin leans conspicuously to the right.

Melissa stops and observes. "Looks like that cabin's too tired to stand up."

"Pulled too many all-nighters," I say.

"Had one too many bourbons." Carl demonstrates by staggering a bit closer with his skis.

Sharon laughs. "I choose D: all of the above."

Carl trudges over to the front porch and looks around. "More likely the foundation's been eaten by termites."

Sharon moves to the window, cupping her hand over her eyes as she peers in.

"What a mess."

"What's in there?" Melissa calls, standing a safe distance away.

"It's dark and hard to tell. A couple of wooden chairs turned over. Garbage."

"Let me have a look." I walk over and take her place at the window.

"Davie, I saw some weird stuff," Sharon whispers, "like chains on the wall."

From the looks of it, this is a one-room cabin. There's an empty space in the center of the room. It's creepy all right. Then I see a large cage in the corner. It's covered with a black cloth. I turn my back to the window to piece my thoughts together. I want to be sure before jumping to any conclusions. But illegal animal fighting comes immediately to mind. Just recently, when the shelter took in a second badger cub, Mr. Marcial talked to us about badger baiting—illegal betting on the outcome of fights between badgers and dogs. It's a cruel sport not seen very often anymore. It was really disturbing. In fact, I have an image that is hard to get out of my mind. Mr. Marcial also reminded us that Mustard, our first badger cub, was found with a broken chain still around his neck.

Carl returns from checking out the perimeter. "You know," he ponders, "this might have been a maintenance shack. Tires need chains for traction in the snow and—"

"I don't think so," I say. "Come take a look."

"Gee, don't tell me." Carl knows exactly what I'm thinking. First he stares at me; then he hesitates and steps to the window. He exhales loudly. "Okay, there's an ashtray with cigarette butts in it. That tells me the cabin's been used recently. And there's a stained towel on a hook. I think … I think it has dried blood on it."

"Come on, let's go," Melissa insists, picking up the vibe. "We'll miss our ride."

"Yeah, right." Sharon joins Melissa, but she looks stricken, preoccupied.

"We're out of here," Carl says, pausing to poke something on the ground with his pole. Looking down, I see a dog's leash caked in mud. That's when I know for sure. Something's up, and dogs are involved. I look at Carl. He knows. His face is a mirror of his dad's when abused animals are rescued. It's a face reserved for the worst scenarios at the Paw Paw Patch. Carl's jaw is clenched as he rolls the leash tightly and stuffs it in his jacket pocket. Then he exhales and meets my eyes. Sharon tugs at my sleeve. She knows. Even Melissa knows what the cabin represents, though she prefers not to talk about it. We all fall completely silent. This will be something to deal with later. That's for certain.

We push off and head down the road. The sun sits on the horizon like a basketball on a rim. The sky to the east is streaked with charcoal.

"It'll be dark soon," Melissa says, clinging to Carl's arm.

"I'll text Avery," Carl says. "He shouldn't be long. Maybe fifteen minutes."

Abruptly, Sharon turns around. "Did you hear that?" Her voice is unusually high-pitched for a tough-it-out kind of girl.

"What?" I pull off my orange hat.

"Listen!" She raises her hand and remains completely still. Up ahead, a group of birds take off in a scattering flurry. I hear the shrieks of a hawk. We've finally reached a main road. I see the flapping of wings. Sharon dashes ahead, waving her hands to scare the hawk away.

"Good Lord!" she exclaims, with a combination of pity and disgust. We are looking at the silent body of a small white-tailed deer. No longer suffering, the dead animal is lying in the snow on the shoulder of the road. A front leg is broken where a bone protrudes from the skin. The tire tracks are from a good-sized truck. The road reveals an all-too-common story. I step from my skis in slow motion. On my knees, I gently cradle the deer's lifeless face. I pet the animal's forehead. I rock. All around me, I sense the spirit of this deer.

"Davie?" Sharon taps my shoulder. Faintly, I can hear Melissa weeping as Carl guides her from the site, assuring her there's nothing to be done. When I stand, there are lights in the distance. Our meeting place is only a hundred yards away. It seems farther. When we arrive, we remove our skis, lean against some boulders, and wait by the sign: "Baraboo Golf Club."

"Traffic on the local roads," Sharon says, "it's really increasing. That's what Grandpa says."

"Yeah," I reply, keeping an eye out for Avery, "particularly trucks. Trucks carrying sand."

"Yeah. Like caravans," Carl says. "Where we live, further west, neighbors have been talking about trucks moving back and forth even on nights and weekends. It's really crappy; the noise never stops—and it's getting worse."

Sharon frowns. "I haven't been paying much attention. Not lately. Missy and I have been sort of dealing with other stuff."

"Yeah," Melissa sighs, "like our dad walking out on Mom, It's horrible. And kind of recent."

"Whoa, that's major," says Carl.

"Lately, besides the shelter," Sharon admits, "it's hard to think about anything else."

"For escape?" Melissa replies. "She skis like a maniac."

Sharon considers this. "Okay, true. It helps. That way my life can't catch up to me."

Melissa looks at Carl. "I was hoping if I didn't mention family stuff, things might go back the way they were."

"That's cool," Carl replies.

"Yeah," Sharon sighs. "Let's not talk about family. Dad's not coming to his senses anytime soon. You can forget that."

"Okay. Subject change!" Melissa calls out. "So—tell me, Carl, what's with all the trucks day and night? We don't have that by us."

"Oh, that," Carl replies. "It all has to do with fracking. Basically, sand *used* for fracking."

"What's the deal with fracking, anyway?" Melissa asks.

Carl looks at me. "Davie's the one to ask."

"It's complicated," I answer, "and controversial, for sure. In a nutshell, fracking is the removal of natural gas—supposedly a cheap method. They are using water and sand to blast apart shale rock and pipe out the gas. Cheaper now maybe, but in the long run—a real threat to our underground water supply. The water we drink!"

"Yeah," Carl adds, "and hello—water is what we're mostly made of."

"Besides," I continue, trying to paint the whole picture, "they're not using any old beach sand, but the quartzite sand found largely here in Southwest Wisconsin."

"Why pick on us?" Sharon asks.

"Seems Wisconsin has the majority of it."

"Lucky us," Carl says.

Melissa puts up her hand to interrupt. "Wait a sec. With things getting busy, won't there be a lot of jobs for people, though? More jobs, more money to go around. Right?" Melissa appears to be having an epic realization. "People can go to the mall. They can shop—buy stuff, cars, houses, clothes." She reaches a crescendo. "Hello! Hey, I could get a real pair of UGGs instead of cheapo imitations."

"Gee," replies Sharon, "thus making the world a much better place."

"Stop it, you two, and listen." I stand still, pretending to be patient, and wait. "I'm giving you both time out." Finally I have their attention. "The sand-mining craze is no joke. Talk about a health hazard. These airborne sand particles can get trapped in your lungs—trapped like forever. There's asthma, cancer, emphysema—you name it."

"Airborne particles?" Carl frowns and instinctively touches his chest. "Where'd you get all these details, Davie?"

"The only source more accurate than the Internet," I answer. "Grandpa."

"He's an environmental encyclopedia," Melissa says. "Kind of glad he doesn't live with us. Too much reality."

"Actually," I admit, "sometimes I hear more than I'd like to. Osmosis, I guess. And science-related newsletters he leaves around everywhere. Like the BSSA."

"What's that?" Sharon asks.

Melissa shrugs. "Sounds like a sports league."

"Not even close," I reply. "It's the bulletin of the Seismological Society of America. They researched not one but a series of earthquakes in Ohio in the spring last year. One hit a magnitude of 3.0, okay? They claim the quake was induced by hydraulic fracking. Plain and simple."

"Whoa!" Carl's eyes are glued to me. "A new fault was created?"

"Not according to Grandpa," I reply. "No. Not a new fault. An *old* fault was reactivated by all the mining." I think back. What did Grandpa say? "Something about a deep, very old layer of the earth. The basement—yeah, the Precambrian basement, he said."

"I'm impressed," Melissa says, staring at me. "You're a sponge, Davie."

"Thanks ... I guess."

"Think of it," Carl says. "What the heck was that sinkhole all about?"

"Pretty strange," Sharon says. "Who knows? I mean, fracking hasn't come to Baraboo. Not yet."

"Right," I reply, "but sand mining has."

"Man." Carl shakes his head. "Mudslides, earthquakes, tremors. Do we really want more of these kinds of things?"

"Get this," Sharon says. "Aunt Martha, Mom's oldest sister, works at a low-income elementary school. It's west of here in Trempeleau County. Seems a mining company set up a site less than a football field away from the classrooms. They claim they have mining rights to frack on the property."

"Well, that's crazy," Carl responds. "That doesn't make sense."

Sharon throws up her hands. "Showed legal papers from a hundred years ago. That's what's happening. Low-income people, it seems, don't have much of a say."

"Or little school kids." Melissa paces back and forth. "Gee, I mean, it's hard to know what to think."

"Well, I'll bet you're not alone," I reply. "The ads on television make fracking sound great. Prosperity, our future, and all that."

Melissa stops pacing and faces us. "You know, to be fair, no two companies are alike. Before Mom got a teaching license, she worked in the office for a well-established mining company. It was a long commute, fifty miles east, but she liked working there. I remember. Aunt Martha dropped me off after school sometimes. They had a lovely walking trail on the grounds. I'd walk there with Mom while Sharon skied all afternoon. We'd watch birds by the marsh on a wooden boardwalk. Loons, wild geese. That's where I saw my first dark-eyed junco."

Coincidentally, Carl's phone tweets. "The charcoal-and-white bird, right?"

Melissa smiles. "Yeah, the one that looks like a chimney sweep." With the flashlight on his phone, Carl signals as Avery rounds the curve. He flashes his high beams twice to let us know he sees us in the fading light. As the van crunches to a careful stop, he rolls down the window.

"Climb up and pile on in. There's a hot meal straight ahead. Real chili and imposter chili for … the attractive alien."

"You mean *vegetarian!*" Melissa laughs and hands me her skis.

Carl and I stuff all the equipment in the roof-topper, and we pile in. Avery waits until we're all buckled in. "Those are some long faces," he says, looking in the rearview mirror. Carl describes the dead deer by the side of the road.

"Sure is a pity," he says, checking the mirror, "but common 'round the city and the 'burbs, ya heh. But, for sure, life on my farm's a different world 'tirely. Quiet pastures, pretty orchards, fields o' wildflowers in the spring. The way it's supposed ta be. Just ask my goat, Tyrone."

Avery does his best to cheer us up with Tyrone stories. How the pet goat ate Avery's favorite wool socks. How he downed a pizza box and a full bag of jalapeño-lime chips. Tired, hungry, and overwhelmed, nobody says much. Avery's eyes are glued to the road as he navigates. His brow wrinkles, and he bites his lip. He's thinking. I look back. There's nothing but darkness behind us. Sharon leans her head against the passenger side window. She's unusually droopy. I suspect that little deer has taken her natural exuberance away. Avery hums.

"Anyone want to stop at the biffy?" he asks. "There's a gas station comin' up."

"Oh yeah," Sharon replies. "I'm ready for a bathroom break."

"Me too," Melissa fake whispers to Sharon. "The gentlemen have left their share of yellow ice behind, I'm sure." Carl and I don't answer.

While the girls use the restroom at the Exxon, Carl informs Avery about the general conditions on the Ice Age Loop. His version is carefully edited until the part about the sinkhole.

"Yep, I can believe it," Avery replies. "County west o' here had one heck of a mudslide after a heavy storm. That was a while back."

"Must have been a lot of rain, huh?" Carl sounds half asleep.

"Had some connection ta sand minin'. You bet'cha. The sand rush is on, and we've got the goods."

The heat in the van puts me into a pleasant kind of daze. We wait for the girls. They return to the van carrying several bags of treats, water, and, of course, a Diet Coke for Melissa. The only sound is the munching of chips and granola bars. When we turn off the main road, Avery perks up. We're only a few miles from home.

"So are you kids ready for tomorrow? Big day, ain' it?"

"The ice-fishing trip? Heck yeah," Carl replies. "Totally psyched!"

Sharon comes alive. "Wouldn't miss it for anything. It's our anything-can-happen day every year."

As we pull into the driveway, Melissa stretches and groans. "Speak for yourself. Ice-fishing—ugh—my yearly punishment."

"Oh, you'll do just fine," Carl says, nudging Melissa. "You'll have a terrific fishing partner." He grins. I feel a twinge of envy at Carl's easy confidence. Wish I could feel as relaxed around girls—ones who aren't my cousins. Avery cracks me up with his charm. He really attempts to interest Melissa in fishing. He's playful but not delusional like Grandpa, who wants his granddaughter to actually *enjoy* fishing.

"Well now, Melissa, the new lures are just beauties, I tell ya."

She humors him. "Would you save the brightest red one for me?"

We pull down the driveway next to Grandpa's beloved old Saab and dash into the house. The aroma of spicy chili has jackets flying. Wearing a long apron, Grandpa waves to us with a wooden spoon in hand.

"Bowls are in here!" he calls before disappearing back into the kitchen. "Sit yourselves down while it's steamin' hot."

In minutes, everyone is totally focused on the food. Plates of cornbread with jalapeño are slathered with butter. With the first spoonful, I realize my appetite is a bottomless pit. The steam from my bowl compounds the heat in my mouth. A delicious fire. The meal tastes better than anything I can recall, especially the hot mulled cider poured into oversize mugs. I'm still wearing my fingerless gloves but nobody seems to notice or care. After a second helping, I close my eyes. My breathing slows down. I'm sinking lower in the chair when Carl taps me on the shoulder.

"Hey, Davie, rise and shine, bro! The table is cleared, and you can fall out on the couch." He nudges me again. "Come on, it's time! Your grandpa and Avery are about to start!"

Carl refers to a family tradition. Storytelling. This ritual is something I look forward to as much as my aunt's chocolate pecan pie. In fact, two of these pies are resting on the side table. I had my eyes on them all through supper—a glaze of pecans, dark chocolate chunks, and a buttery crust. I choose the floor by the fire as everyone else finds a comfortable place.

Folding my hands under my chin, elbows out, I lie on a full and happy stomach. The difficulties of the day seem to fade away like the pages in a chapter I've already finished.

Of course, I've heard Avery's tales many times over. They're always a touch different, with added details, a new character, a suspenseful twist. Avery is part Ojibwa, a tribe of Native Americans from around Wisconsin and the Great Lakes. His stories, mostly ancient myths and folktales, have always gripped me. I recall a time when I was too young to understand that his stories are fiction.

A chill runs through me suddenly. This is one night when I can't get close enough to the fire. I look around self-consciously. I sense my palm. Burning again. I wiggle my fingers. Squeeze my hand a few times, look around. Sharon is melded to a big stuffed chair, her feet tucked under a wool throw. Melissa and Carl are stretched out together on the L-shaped couch. I press my hand to a cool square of tile on the floor. My paw print, a hidden brand—a reminder.

I wonder what lies ahead. For the moment, I feel almost invisible. I have a freeing sense of anonymity. My mind slowly empties. My eyes return to the hypnotic orange glow, the lapping flames. Turning my face toward the fire, I see the sculptured shape of a badger in the shadowy logs. I blink and let my gaze follow. Outside is yet another reminder; I hear the lonely sound of tree branches scraping the roof like claws. Instantly, my hand searches for the smooth green stones in my pocket. They're soothing, cool. I sense movement, energy. Even as the burning fades, I know. The badgers' strange and baffling gift is not inert. I feel the promise of adventure in my fingertips.

7

TALES BY THE FIRE

Grandpa John pops up out of his chair. "Avery, I just about forgot. Why, I promised I would break out that special brandy. Helps fortify. Had it so long it probably aged in the darn bottle. Maybe I can find those snifters I stashed away. Hold on, kids, won't take but a minute."

"Well then, I'll lend a hand," offers Avery, stopping his rocking chair. "Hold on there."

"Nah, you go on and stay put, Avery!"

"Cripes, John, I don't need for you ta wait on me. I'm not old enough ta be pampered, ya heh! Got a bad knee is all. I kin walk."

"Oh, pipe down. Pretend you're my guest."

"No sirree. How long have we known each other? What—forty some years? Fifty?" Avery follows Grandpa into the kitchen, limping slightly and mumbling just loud enough so I can hear. "Just don't badger me about my knee."

"'Badger me.'" Right. A nice idiom, that's all it is. I refuse to get all worked up. The truth is they badger each other constantly, but always in fun. So different, yet one and the same. Of course, they both use the local twang. 'Sconsin talk, I call it. As for their friendship, all the basics are there. There's history, loyalty, and trust. Back in the early seventies, they fought in Vietnam together. "'If the metal holding my leg together were gold, Davie, I'd be one rich cheddarhead!'" ("cheddarhead" being a nickname for Wisconsinites—like it or not). They met working the cranberry bogs over in Tomah the summer before they were drafted.

45

They were young, like nineteen or so, when the army shipped them off to fight in Vietnam. Grandpa received a bad concussion that knocked him cold and damaged his hearing. He insists that if it weren't for Avery, he'd be a goner. Avery was wounded carrying him out of the line of fire. Luckily, a helicopter medevacked them to an army hospital. When the war ended, they came home. Grandpa went to college. Avery worked the dairy farm owned by his extended family. Still does. Grandpa is the scientist; Avery, the farmer. Grandpa is the activist; Avery, the dramatist. Bottom line, they're tight like brothers.

I glance over at Sharon, Carl, and Melissa. I'm dead tired yet wide awake. I keep seeing that spiral in the snow. The striped faces. The full moon. I'll go crazy if I don't come clean, tell them everything. I'll explode like a meteor hitting the earth. That's it. Tonight is the time—the perfect opportunity to arrange a secret meaning. Grandpa and Avery are still in the kitchen. They'll be asleep by ten o'clock at the latest. In a loud whisper, I take the plunge.

"Hey. Listen up guys! Something major has come up." I nod toward the kitchen. "I'm talking *classified*. Totally. We need to meet tonight up in the attic. Ten o'clock. Not one word."

Nobody says a thing. They look at each other, then back at me. I'm about to repeat myself when Carl nods. Sharon puts up ten fingers, and Melissa gives a thumbs-up. At that exact moment, as if on cue, the wind howls outside with a high-pitched whining sound, rattling the windows. My timing couldn't be better.

"Gee, who's doing the sound effects?" Sharon asks, walking to the window and peering through the blind. "Sounds like we're live and on location,"

"You heard Grandpa," Melissa replies. "He says it could be like ten degrees tomorrow."

"Tops. It's bound to be even colder with the windchill."

"Davie's right," Sharon says. "But I have total faith you'll rise to the occasion, Missy. You'll just have to dress in layers. And you have plenty of those."

"You'll just have to stay really, really close." Carl winks and draws

Melissa against his chest. She snuggles against him and smiles before she resumes pouting again. I have to admit she's beautiful, but she's also completely high-maintenance.

"Problem is," Melissa groans, "I'm already tired of snow! And, of course, what is tomorrow? Officially the first day of winter. The *first* day."

Sharon moves right in. A reality check. "Come on. You're just in a funk because of Dad."

"Maybe."

"Forget maybe. You are." Sharon explains it in three words: "He's wrecked everything."

"Yeah, he sure has. We're not speaking. He's hurt Mom."

"The man's toast."

"You mean burned toast."

"I can't believe Dad moved into that condo with what's-her-name."

"*Wheatley.*"

"Sounds like an overpriced cereal, right?"

"An underage cereal!" Melissa pauses. "She's *a lot* younger."

"*Beaucoup* younger!" Sharon echoes. "But it won't last long."

Melissa laughs harshly. "Trust me—she won't like his no-frills condo."

"Correct. Shh! Here they come."

Avery leads carrying two snifters of brandy, while Grandpa John slowly follows balancing a tray holding a birthday cake, candles flaming. Fifteen candles. When everyone joins in singing, I feel my face flush with genuine surprise. I'd almost forgotten. I make a wish and blow out the candles. I pick up the knife but hesitate to cut the cake. Like a kid, I don't want to ruin the white stars of the Winter Hexagon on top of the blue frosting. Before I cut the first slice, Carl takes a picture with his phone. Then Sharon distributes forks, napkins, and generous slices.

"Mom made it from scratch," Melissa says. "Consider yourself hugged."

"It's awesome."

"We made Grandpa our accomplice." Sharon laughs. "He took a picture of your ceiling to the bakery."

"Yep," Grandpa replies, "it's hard to keep a secret around here."

If he only knew. The hairs stand up on the back of my neck. Silently, I finish my cake.

"Well now," begins Avery, "by the looks of it, I think my story may last longer than this here fine brandy!" He tastes it and nods with satisfaction. I notice his hands, flecked with brown spots, knuckles swollen from working the cranberry bogs and doing farm chores in every kind of weather. "But it's an old story, you bet'cha. Much older than these fine spirits." Avery swirls the amber liquid and sniffs the aroma. He nods and begins. "North o' the Great Lakes, where tales have trickled down like a slow-movin' creek—that's where my people come from. As tales get told, why, they change some, get passed on. Takes time, ya heh. But they're remembered, not forgotten; that's the way of the Ojibwa, my people." Avery angles his rugged face toward the firelight. He tucks his hands behind his head, elbows out, and rocks without another word. We wait. When he's ready, his deep, resonant voice fills the room. His pause, like a rising curtain, already has us in its silent grip.

"Now, my great-uncle had only one ear. I never asked why, mind ya, 'cause I was afraid ta ask. He told me stories about a place he called the North Country. Claims there was a creature up there, a monster with strange powers, livin' and hidin' under the ground. Yep. Whatever *it* was attacked and left no traces. People got mighty scared when hunters never returned home. Experienced hunters just disappeared. Along the shores, canoes were found empty." He lowers his voice to a whisper. "Abandoned."

"Abandoned?" Carl wonders aloud. "But no footprints, you say. That's sort of impossible, isn't it?"

"You tell me. Not a trace." Avery rocks. "But there were rumors. Lotsa rumors."

"Like?" Sharon asks.

"Based on what?" Melissa gives us her know-it-all look. "Gossip?"

"More like … terror," Avery replies. "Sheer terror of the unknown."

"But…"

"Shh!" I hiss. "Let him finish."

"Some said a horned water snake was ta blame. So, as protection, an offerin' of tobacco was common practice, thrown into the water." Avery takes another slow sip. "Well, the people finally decide shape-shifting must be involved. And, ya see, as a result, they become very suspect of strangers. They keep their eyes open for people that don't belong. Through time, mind ya, they become careful guardians of their territory. Ya could say watchdogs."

"Speaking of which," Melissa suggests, "good reason to keep a German shepherd or a Doberman."

"Might not have worked," Avery replies without smiling.

"Why not?" Carl asks. "Sounds logical to me."

"Some claimed the creature could make itself invisible simply by turnin' sideways. Real sneaky like. Couldn't see it comin'! Others said the creature would burrow into the sand and wait like a trap-door spider. Then strike!"

"How did they finally catch it?" Sharon asks.

"*They* didn't." Avery pauses for emphasis. "*She* did."

"She?" Sharon asks.

"A brave young woman. A girl your age, mind ya. She tricked the monster into facin' her dead on."

"How?"

"Why, with the spell—the spell of her green eyes! Light green, like yours, in fact."

"Avery, get out!" Sharon scoffs. "You're so making this up."

"Personally, I'd be beyond petrified," Melissa confesses, sitting forward on the couch. "And this girl wasn't even afraid?"

"Not afraid? My girl, she was *terrified*! But that didn't stop her, ya heh. Fear is only fear. She had something more."

"What?" Sharon asks. "Like a weapon?"

"Better than any weapon. She had courage!"

"That's it?" Disappointed, I sit straight up. I feel cheated. "That'll only take you so far, Avery."

"Well now," Avery admits, looking right at me, "courage played a part. But, in fact, she was helped by a magical stone she carried with her."

I feel transparent. Frozen. Speechless.

"Go on," Carl says. "What happens next?"

"Well, this is the part o' the story where my great-uncle would stop."

"Stop?" Carl practically shouts. "Why would he stop now?"

"Well," replies Avery, mischievously, "so I would eat my vegetables."

"Avery!"

Carl, Melissa, and Sharon whine, coax, and laugh at the same time. I say nothing. Do nothing. I turn and stare into the fire, my back to everyone. My heart is racing as if I'd had three cups of Grandpa's extreme coffee.

"Avery hasn't even gotten to the best part yet," Grandpa says.

Melissa ups the stakes. "Avery, you're killing us!"

"Psychological torture," Sharon groans.

"Cruel and usual punishment, Avery." Carl crosses his arms, waiting expectantly for the finale.

"You can't stop here," Melissa adds. "It's … illegal."

"All right, then." Avery lowers his voice to a whisper. "If you think you can take it." Another sip. "So, with the green stone in hand, the girl somehow grows taller and taller. At last, she's face-to-face with the enemy. Then it becomes clear. She alone cannot win." Avery swirls the remains of the brandy and empties his glass. We wait. "That, my friends, is part one." Then he sighs and closes his eyes, and it's clear our storyteller is done for the night. Like a television series, Avery cleverly excuses himself at eight thirty, promising a rain check on his story. "Sorry ta be a party pooper, ya heh. Hate ta leave you in the lurch, but I was up all last night with a sick animal. Yep, our oldest dairy cow, Elvira. She'll make it, but, Lord, will I?" He chuckles, stands unsteadily. "Professor, take over for me." Avery heads down the hall. "Once your grandpa gets started, kids, he'll bend yer ear till the fish stop bitin' and the sun goes down."

Avery opens the door to a cozy guest room that has a comfortable futon in it. He waves good night.

Grandpa hangs in for quite a while. In that time, he manages to answer a lot of our questions. I have the first.

"What do you know about Devil's Lake? The history and stuff."

"Well, let's see," Grandpa ponders. "Where to start …"

"Way far back!" Melissa demands.

"Back then, this whole area of Wisconsin was a giant inland ocean."

"Grandpa," Sharon asks doubtfully, "an ocean here—like with waves, tides, sandy beaches?"

"Yep. That's a fact. The bluffs of Baraboo are ancient."

"How ancient?" Carl asks.

"Oh, just a *billion* years old." Now Grandpa is on a roll. "Then, more recently, over two and a half *million* years ago, colossal ice sheets came and went. That's your Ice Age. That ended with an extreme event. The big one: the Wisconsin Glacier."

"I love the word 'event,'" Melissa says. "Not like there was anyone around to party."

"You're right there," Sharon replies. "No fashion fundraisers."

"Okay, so here we go. Timeline." Grandpa's face comes alive. He looks like a quarterback running with the ball. "Picture one part, the Green Bay lobe, partly blocked by the bluffs, held off and advancing over the east end of the Baraboo Hills, and then slicing through into both ends of Devil's Lake Gorge!"

"Wow," Carl says. "Cool. The quarterback sneak. The glacier cuts through to score—a lake."

An important connection is now clear to me. "Devil's Lake?"

"You bet'cha." Grandpa stands up. He's in professor mode. "And a whole lot more. That one glacier changed the face of North America."

"You're not kidding, Grandpa," Melissa responds. "That's extreme all right. Kind of like plastic surgery."

"Oh please." Sharon snorts.

Grandpa moves to the wall and gestures on an imaginary map. "That's why we have the Great Lakes, the Ohio River, and even Niagara Falls; and that's just the tip o' the iceberg."

"Masterful pun, Grandpa." I give a thumbs-up. Grandpa acknowledges this, but then, just as quickly, his smile fades. He sighs deeply. "But it all comes down to this. This is when our quarter of Wisconsin was left with very heavy sand deposits. Quartzite sand."

I dive in. "Sorry if I spilled milk on yesterday's newspaper, Grandpa. I got mad when I saw the headline: 'Wisconsin, Sandbox of the Nation.'"

"Scary, wasn't it?"

"For sure. I got the jist," I answer. "Seems we're unlucky enough to have the perfect sand everybody wants."

"You got it," Grandpa replies. "Frac sand."

"Lucky us," Carl says.

"That's a discussion that'll have ta wait." Grandpa stretches and yawns. "But at least I know who crumpled my newspaper." He stands and winks. "I need to pack it in. Ice fishin' tomorrow. See ya at the crack o' dawn." He heads down the hall. "Remember—emphasis on *dawn*. Good night, kids."

I stand up and plop down on the couch. "Grandpa's a whirlwind, isn't he?"

"Tell me about it," Sharon answers with a laugh. "You're a lot like him."

"Oh, get out."

"Really. You have his large brain."

"I wish."

"He's totally awesome," Carl states. "Can I adopt him?"

In his pajamas and robe, Grandpa reappears for a glass of water in the kitchen. Then, slippers smacking on the floor, he heads back to his bedroom at the far end of the hall. I picture his room. It's a total trip. Right now he's probably stepping over boxes filled with papers and notes; enough, really, to merit the title "archives." Under his bed are more boxes—the long, clear plastic kind—filled with volumes of stuff. Literally. Old copies of the *Canadian Geotechnical Journal* and the *Bulletin of Engineering Geology and the Environment*. Geologists retire, but they're still geologists. That's obvious. His endless bookshelves rise to the ceiling, crowded with textbooks, essays, reference books, *Audubon* and *National Geographic*. That's just for starters, and that's just one wall. It goes on. There is no wallpaper; only maps that cover every inch of wall except for the clock. The best feature of all is the unique dartboard, which identifies all the sand-mining operations in Wisconsin. There used to be three. Now there are over a hundred. Grandpa keeps his sense of humor about it, though. "That's pretty sad," he once said to me, "but it does make for a better game of darts."

His door closes. Check. My sense of anticipation is unbearable. I feel like it's New Year's Eve in Times Square and a ball is dropping through my skull. The ashes barely glimmer. The fire is almost out. Check. It's dead quiet until the clock on the upstairs landing comes alive. A tiny door opens. The little yellow cuckoo announces ten o'clock. Check. Our signal to assemble. By the tenth chirp, Carl, Melissa, and Sharon meet me on the landing. With our shoes off, we tiptoe up the creaky oak staircase to the attic.

8
THE ATTIC

The musty smell of old things hits me as I slowly twist the doorknob.

"Smells like Dad's antique shop up here." Sharon wrinkles her nose.

Melissa sniffs. "Antiques? High-class junk, you mean."

"That's really good. 'High-class junk.' We should suggest that name to him."

Melissa exhales very slowly. Her frustration could blow open the door. "I'm sure his girlfriend, Wheatley, will be a terrific business partner."

The door creaks open. I almost trip on a shoebox full of index cards. "Whatever wouldn't fit in Grandpa's room when he moved in. It's all here."

"That was, like, ages ago, Davie." Sharon scans the mountains and piles of stuff. "Wasn't it?"

"Four years, about. I helped cart this stuff up here."

"Child labor," Carl laughs.

I pummel him. "Who you calling a child, Carlito?"

"Smells a bit like the stable at the Paw-Paw," Carl adds, "after the famous flood."

"Get out," I reply. "Nothing could be worse than that."

"Whew," Sharon complains, "mildew."

"Black lung." Melissa covers her mouth with her hand.

"Shh!" I scold. "Enough. Cut it out." I'm feeling edgy. There's stuff weighing on my mind. The badgers.

We enter the large, unlit attic. I turn on my phone's flashlight.

Bookshelves of all sizes rest in the odd-shaped nooks and crannies. The attic is maxed out. A tsunami of out-of-print geology textbooks, tons of nonfiction, maps in oversized manila folders, and a huge series on National Parks in America stretches from end to end. On the floor, dozens of covered plastic boxes marked "rock samples" make it challenging to walk a straight line.

"Yucky," Melissa gasps. "Call Air Quality Control."

Sharon picks up a book. "Just stop breathing."

"Too late." Melissa blows against her palm. "It's so cold up here I can see my breath."

In one corner, a white porcelain bathtub rests on its claw feet like a giant soap dish. Carl finds the switch on the ceramic heater and turns it on full blast. Sharon, rubbing her hands together, follows the moonlight to the four narrow windows. They make me think of *Romeo and Juliet*, each one pushing outward.

Sharon's face is lit. I join her at the window. "Quite a moon, huh?"

"Yeah," she replies, "it looks larger than normal."

Carl comes over with an old mop. "Giant basketball." We move aside while he removes hanging cobwebs from the broad sill. It hits me. When I was younger, I used to come up here all the time to poke around. My computer changed all that—and video games, my old telescope, my job. In fact, I'm surprised the batteries in the rusty camp lantern are still good. Carl still manages to knock into a pile of worn-out doggie beds. The pet beds are large, having belonged to Grandpa's Plott hound, Terrence. That was back when the dog and I were the same size. I choose a lumpy red velvet cushion and plop down.

"Good old Terrence." Sharon sits down beside me on a rectangular plaid cushion. It's large enough for her to curl up on. Melissa squeezes next to Carl on the red-and-black-check oval I vividly remember. For a moment, I'm a little boy touring Parfrey's Glen refuge with Grandpa, sad because we couldn't take Terrence with us. Suddenly I'm choked up. My eyes start to water. I have to shake off a sudden urge to cry, just as I did back then. Instead I bring the big, loving brown eyes and giant paws into focus. I take a big breath and start.

"Are we good?" I glance around to see everyone waiting expectantly.

"This is strange. It's freaky, but it's okay." This isn't the best intro. "So here's the deal." I look from Carl to Sharon to Melissa, afraid they won't take me seriously. I put up my hands like I'm being arrested and pause. I peel off my fingerless black glove, checking my palm first to make sure the mark is still there. Five claws. Warily, I reverse my hand and reveal the badger paw print.

To get a closer look, Carl grabs my wrist. "What the heck …"

"Jeez," Sharon says, "what exactly is going …"

Melissa's voice is like an accusation. "Come on, Davie, where did you …"

I try to read their faces as, one by one, they examine my hand. It's unanimous. They don't know what to make of it. Not surprising. Their eyes are wide with more than a touch of doubt. Suspicion is more accurate. Carl motions for silence. They wait like puppies. I'm holding the treats.

"Have you tried scrubbing it off?" Melissa reaches out gingerly to touch my palm. She does, and quickly draws back.

"Can't wash it off. I've tried; believe me."

Sharon tilts her head, wondering, of course, if this is a practical joke. She takes a tissue from her pocket and spits on it, eyeing me with distrust. "Permanent marker, right?"

"Wrong."

Forcefully, like a vice, she grabs my hand and rubs hard. Spits, rubs, spits, and rubs.

"Hey, that's gross," I object.

"Just making sure."

"Don't say anything yet, okay?" I control my frustration and dry my palm. "Please, just listen!" I'm not sure I like the three pairs of skeptical eyeballs on me right now. "In the middle of the night—crazy early, like I'm enjoying some REM—two badgers, striped faces and all, came by for a little visit. Their movement set off the outside lights." Melissa raises her eyebrows. Sharon clears her throat. I ignore it. "I'm practically delirious when they sit—no, *park* themselves, okay—under my window."

"Badgers? You're sure? Not skunks?" Carl asks. "Just that … well, it'd be more likely."

"Totally not skunks, Carl. I know my skunks." I pause. "They looked like my grandpa's shaving brush, okay?" Carl laughs. I continue. "There was a full-size badger and a smaller one—male and female, I'm assuming. They tracked me with their eyes! It was freaky. Of course, they backed off when I crept outside. That's when I saw it—the shape in the snow."

"Wait. A shape?" Sharon asks, with disturbing scrutiny. She usually takes my side in things. Right now I'd like to pop her in her wrinkled nose. Her face looks pale in the light. If she creases her brow any more, she'll look like a snowshoe rabbit. "Come on, Davie. You're saying ... these badgers weren't just ... digging?"

"No! They were not just digging."

"Come on," Melissa coaxes. "Cut it out, Davie."

Maybe I expected this kind of reaction, but that doesn't make it less annoying. "Hear me out. We're talking a *shape*. A spiral—a definite spiral."

"Isn't it possible," Melissa counters, "that was just an accidental kind of thing."

My voice rises. My patience is going. "Uh, no. It was deliberate. Not an accident." I struggle to be nice. "The design was too perfect." Carl is listening intently. At least he seems with me.

"Hey, let Davie finish, okay?"

I reach for the evidence. "What's more, there were four stones in the very center."

"Stones?" Sharon looks puzzled. "That not strange around here, is it?"

"See for yourself! These are anything *but* ordinary stones." My confidence returns as I wave them back and forth in my palm.

"Green stones," Carl replies, reaching for one. "Could be mossy or ..." He rubs the stone. "Never mind." He holds the stone to the light. The iridescent particles shimmer inside. "Whoa. You're not kidding. It's like—like nothing I've ever seen before."

The stones are passed around. I feel elated, as though I've just won a Nobel Prize. I sit back on my dog bed and cross my legs.

"Hold on. Wait a sec." With a look of concern, Sharon reaches down. She touches her ankle. "Something feels weird." With a frown, she narrows her eyes. "What the ..." Very slowly, apprehensively, she pulls off her untied boot and rolls down her thick woolen sock. She freezes. On her ankle bone is a mark identical to mine. "No way! This is ... crazy."

"Come into the light." Carl moves the lantern up against her leg.

"Yeah," he murmurs, "same as Davie's."

Melissa protests as though she's uncovered some kind of bizarre plot. "Davie and Sharon! You really had me, you sneaky little toads!" She shakes her head. "You actually did it!"

"Did what?" Sharon says, her hand still on her ankle. "I didn't *do* anything!"

Melissa gives Sharon and me one of her condescending, all-knowing looks and stands up. "You both hitched a ride and got tattoos without—I can't believe it—without even telling me or Carl. You stinkers!" She now boxes me with her mitten and laughs. "So ... where'd you go? When was this?"

"Whoa!" I cut her short. "Stop and listen, will you? I swear on—on Terrence's memory. Sharon and I did not get tattoos!"

"This is no joke," Sharon says. "It's ... I don't know—"

"Something incredibly important," I finish, voicing my gut feeling. How do I convey an instinct so strong it's impossible not to act on it? I collect the green stones. "We're marked." It comes out in a whisper. I clear my throat. "We've been chosen."

"Chosen?" Carl cracks his knuckles. "I think you've been up too long without sleep, bro." Loyalties keep changing. I'm disappointed.

"Davie's on to something," Sharon acknowledges, rubbing her ankle. "It's real. I mean, we have to deal with it. At least find an explanation."

"Well. I am wondering." Melissa now points at the stones but refuses to touch them. "Why *four* stones?" She hesitates, glancing from me to Sharon. "Why not just *two* stones?"

Carl cracks his knuckles again.

Melissa reacts. "Carl, stop! You're making me jumpy."

"Sorry." He stands and paces. "Think logically. Why four stones? Can it be because—because *we* are four?" Carl's strong muscular frame casts a giant shadow on the floor. "So I should have a mark too, then?" He shrugs.

"Don't even say that!" Melissa gives Carl a gentle shove. "No way! You know Davie and Sharon are totally playing us."

Carl raises his sweatpants and checks his ankles. "Nothing, see?" Before Melissa can object, Carl raises his turtleneck so the ripples of his abs are showing. I make a silent vow to take up weight lifting.

"Come on now," Carl says calmly. "Take a close look, Missy. Let's resolve this. I promise, it's going to be okay."

"Only 'cause Carl says so," Melissa objects, yanking my flashlight. She eyes me suspiciously. "But I'm not liking this one bit."

"Nothing there," she says flatly, after checking Carl's chest and sleek waistline, "except a very handsome six-pack." Carl yanks his sweater higher and removes it entirely. Melissa drops the flashlight.

"Better check my neck and back." Carl turns around.

Melissa gasps. "Oh no! Between your shoulder blades—the mark is there!"

"At least I didn't have to drop my drawers," Carl says matter-of-factly. "Same mark?"

Melissa looks panicked. "The paw print thing with five claws."

I take the flashlight, hold it in place while Melissa hovers. "Yeah, that's it."

Sharon half smiles. "Welcome to our world, Carl. Now ..."

Melissa takes a defensive step back. "No you don't. Don't anyone come near me!" Covering her face with her hands, she breaks into a nervous laugh and starts to hyperventilate.

"Melissa, listen," Carl says, shivering as he puts his shirt on. "Just breathe normally." He squeezes her hand.

"I'm scared." Melissa closes her eyes tightly. She tenses her body but lets Sharon approach. "Is it there? Do you see it?"

"Nope ... nope ... you're good." Sharon searches carefully, taking her time. "I can't find any sign of it," Sharon replies, with a sigh. "Your perfect body is fine. More than fine, actually—which is why I hate you." We all laugh. Melissa is smoothing her hair when the realization registers on Sharon's face. Slowly, she lifts her sister's long hair. "The nape of your neck ..."

The mark is there.

9

THE WINTER HEXAGON

I'm expecting Melissa to cry and get all weird on us. But she doesn't. In fact, she breaks from Carl and sits down without the usual drama. We join her and wait.

"It's okay," she says, "really okay." She looks down and pulls lint from the dog bed as she talks. "This is the way I figure it. One, I don't want to be left out. Two, Baraboo is a scenic place to live. But come on, is it brimming with excitement?"

"It's not New York City," Sharon answers, "if that's what you mean." She cocks her head like a terrier. "But then, you can't ski down Fifth Avenue or go ice fishing in Central Park, can you?" I'm liking like this positive shift.

"So then," Melissa continues, "if Davie's hunch is right, this badger thing might lead to something cool. Like an adventure." Her amber eyes light up. "A mysterious one at that."

"No doubt," I acknowledge, staring at my palm. "A journey into the unknown."

"Besides," Melissa adds, lightening up, "I need to fill a gap. Seventh Avenue and the Fashion District are five years away for me." She sounds like she means it.

Sharon is cautious. "Are you for real?"

"Absolutely. I'm good."

"Like helping out at the Patch," Carl reasons, "I think we all agree it feels good to be needed." He realizes we're all waiting for him to go on. "What?"

I fill in. "Of course, at this point we don't know what the badgers need from us. Not yet, anyway."

"Those four stones," Sharon offers, "obviously they're clues." She holds out her hand. "Let's really examine them."

Each, upon careful scrutiny, appears slightly different from the others. They vary in size, shape, and shade of green. The others follow me to the window. Moonlight beams in, illuminating the stones. Particles floating inside remind me of living cells seen under a microscope. Each of us picks a stone. Carl chooses the largest.

"Strange." He checks it out from every angle. "Hmm. No rock I can identify. For sure, it's not from around here."

Melissa chooses the lightest shade. She has her own take. "How lovely. Just like stained glass."

"Like something I'd see in the window of a fine jewelry store," Sharon says, admiring a stone that has the cut facets of a gemstone. "This looks like Mom's birthstone, a peridot."

Carl shakes his stone. "There are moving particles inside!"

My stone is symmetrical in shape. Instinctively, I place it over the mark. A tingling sensation changes to heat. My pulse quickens as I realize the stone is a hexagonal prism. At that very moment, the Winter Hexagon forms on the cloudy lens of my mind. I'm overwhelmed, lost in thoughts of last night: the telescope; the six constellations, the brightest stars in the sky. How do I put this all together?

"I'm holding a hexagon," I say, partly to myself. "A hexagon."

As we compare the stones, my mind whirls with unanswered questions. *We are—the four or us—incredibly different people. Why pick us? What is the mission?*

I ask the inevitable question. "What do we all have in common?"

"Bad grades in French," Melissa quips.

"Nope," I insist, "I take Spanish." I try to keep my cool. "Come on, you guys—for real."

"We work together on Saturdays," Sharon says.

Carl shrugs. "We love animals."

"We're all fifteen?" Melissa looks hopeful. I'm thinking she's onto something.

"Yes—but something else. Something … more." I gesture toward the windows.

Through separate panes, we stare out at the moon.

"Look at the size of that moon." Tonight, I figure, it's even more impressive without a telescope. "It's a beauty, huh?"

Carl's resonant voice adds to the spell. "La luna."

"Perfect," Sharon says. "What Carl means is we're a bunch of lunatics."

"Absolutely," I answer, my face pressed to the glass. "Lunatics were people possessed by the moon, right?"

"Possessed?" Melissa says. "Kept in asylums, I'm sure. Let that be a lesson, people."

As for me, I keep my eyes locked on the moon. I'm still not sure what I'm looking for. In the background, I hear funny interpretations of "lunatic."

"*Lune attic*," Sharon says. "French for 'crazy people in the attic.'"

"That's a chocolate Moon Pie." Carl sounds possessed. "I must have it!"

"Hardly," Melissa objects. "It looks like Gouda. I know my cheeses."

Carl makes an announcement. "On Wisconsin! Cheddarheads unite!"

Cackles of laughter and complete lunacy resonate in the room. Carl has lost it. He wipes his eyes and holds his stomach, trying to get control.

"Hey, seriously, Davie, why *is* the moon so big tonight?"

"It just *appears* larger tonight, Carlito. That's due to its position."

"That's it?" Carl sounds disappointed.

"That's it." I think again. I don't want to diss the moon. "Actually though, the Earth's moon *is* very large compared to the planet it orbits."

Carl is pleased. "So our moon rocks—compared to other moons in the solar system."

"Yeah."

Sharon elbows me. "You know, Davie, now I feel proud of our moon."

"Sure, go ahead. Be proud."

"Moon pride," Melissa says, trying out her slogan.

"I wish I could video this," Carl insists, "but they'd put us all away."

I grab their attention. "Don't forget. This is the year of the thirteenth moon."

"Thirteenth?" Sharon looks at me like I have a third eye in my forehead. "Twelve months, twelve moons, right?"

"Yes and no." I decide to pass on words like "perigee" and "libration." I stick to simple terms. "In our calendar, some months have fewer days. So every few years there are actually not twelve but thirteen full moons. You're looking at number thirteen."

Melissa, turning toward me, looks concerned. "Does that make it unlucky?"

Her question hangs in the air, while my eyes dart to a familiar circle of light on the ground below. I freeze. My heart rumbles. I feel the cold glass on my forehead as I strain to see the outlines. Two badgers. Wide bodies and funny ears. Striped faces looking up at the window.

"Rodents spotted!" Melissa whispers, "O-M-G!"

"They're *Mustelids*."

"Excusez-moi!" Melissa responds, "*Mustelids*, sorry. Gee, Davie, don't lose your lens."

"Wait, that's it." Carl has a brainstorm. "The stones—let's call them musta luminae!"

"I like it." Sharon replies. "Cool."

Melissa agrees. "Musta luminae. That's a perfect name. Davie?"

"A keeper."

I snap my fingers and point outside. "Holy … I'd say they've come for us."

"Not good. My window's fogging!" Hurriedly, Sharon rubs on the glass. "Come on, push open the windows …"

Our breath makes clouds in the cold air. We watch, stunned, as four laser beams of light fly from the badgers' eyes. Green light. These rays find us. They seem connected, programmed somehow to the four musta luminae. The brightness hurts my eyes, but I manage to climb onto the window ledge and balance. In seconds, Carl and Sharon are to the right of me. Melissa is to my left. We thrust the windows open at ninety-degree angles to the house.

"Climb up," I say. "These windows are our portals!"

"Hold on, wait for me! I've got the longest legs," Melissa objects as I help her up.

"I'm good," she says breathlessly, "but I can't look down." I look over to see her hand shaking. But, to her credit, she grips her stone as if it is a plane ticket to NYC. I feel the mark pulse on my palm, growing from warm to hot.

"My mark is activating," I call out. "Your marks will, too. I'm positive. Cross your arms to the center of your chest. Hold tight. Whatever you do, don't let go of the musta luminae." With those words, I feel myself drawn like a magnet from the solid window base, spiraling effortlessly into the air. The sensation is nothing short of miraculous. In one instant, I become a whirling corkscrew piercing the night. We move as one. As I soar, I can sense the parallel energy of my companions. We sail over the lawn, above the fields of snow. I feel as if I am peering out the wrong end of my binoculars; down below the bluffs get smaller and smaller. The tall evergreens fade away. The pines and spruces disappear in a wild blur, branches becoming lines, needles becoming dashes, cones becoming dots.

I feel intensely alert, thrilled beyond imagining with the experience of flight—flight known to me only in dreams of space exploration, of zipping from planet to planet. I barely wonder or care where we are heading. Mystery is totally okay with me. The badgers have given us powers. Parallel to my buddies, I spiral along this laser pathway. I strain unsuccessfully to open my eyes. All I can make out is the vague color green surrounding me. This green vapor must provide a protective barrier, because although I'm surrounded by frigid air, I feel entirely comfortable. It's clear the badgers are guiding us. I trust them just as surely as they trust us with their magical stones. To my amazement, my mark serves as a GPS, alerting me to the location of my buddies. Even with my eyes shut, I can sense their parallel location. None of us have learner's permits; but here we are, twisting along on this crazy four-lane roadway in the sky.

As the bluffs of Baraboo recede, I feel sure we will make a contribution; a difference. And as the heat of the paw print intensifies, I feel it even more. I know with certainty we are partners with the badgers in a powerful, unfolding drama. Directed by a force beyond ourselves, we will play our parts. The subject at the very center of it all: our home, planet Earth. The theme: its preservation.

The Winter Hexagon
(created with Stellarium)

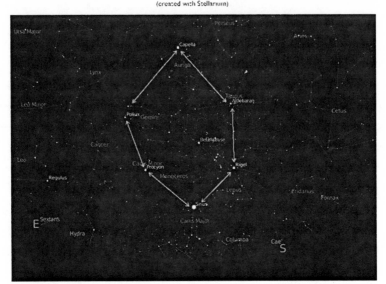

10

SPIRULATION

I'm a beautiful touchdown pass, whirling over streams and ponds. Down below, hibernating frogs lie suspended in frozen beds of mud. "Spirulation"—that's the only name for this wild ride. It knocks me out just to imagine we could be blurs across someone's telescope right now! I get why Sharon loves ski jumping. I get why she loves to slalom at breakneck speed. This is it. To defy gravity even for a little while, that's the ticket. To defy fear.

With the fantastic skills of a bat, I move along. My internal GPS seems to be operating through some kind of echolocation. Carl, Sharon, and Melissa are sending signals back to me. They remain completely parallel to me, moving at the same speed. From dusty dog beds minutes ago, we're soaring. I imagine the badgers have activated the green stones by means of the laser. Not by coincidence, each of us has one musta lumina in possession. I'm reminded of the push-button ignition on Harriet and George's new sedan—the keyless entry, the ability to start the car with the keys anywhere in the vicinity.

I've been going full speed since early this morning. Yet as we zoom toward this unknown destination, I feel fully alert, charged with renewed energy. I have trust. Badgers are, after all, the planners and the architects of the animal world—the construction engineers. I'm totally confident they have a landing site carefully planned.

Rotating faster now, my body isn't my own. My jumbled thoughts diminish as if I'm moving into a lower gear on my bike. My mind empties.

As I decelerate, the ground below me suddenly comes into focus. *Whoosh!* I glide forward in slow motion with impressive control. Abruptly, I feel my body reverse so that my feet are now leading. With relief, I hear the crunch of ground beneath my feet. And as the pull of gravity takes over, I feel my legs preparing, anticipating the ground, my spine lengthening. Still in motion, I hit the ground at a run and come to a smooth stop in a clearing.

Simultaneously, Carl, Sharon, and Melissa land parallel to me. They land safely. To their expressions of surprise and exhilaration, I brush icicles from my hair. Breathlessly, we hug each other. Continuously, we jump up and down. Like Super Bowl winners, we do a spontaneous cheer. As the wonder of it all registers, we morph into a huddle, our hands on each other's shoulders. We're high up on a ridge, and the air smells sweet and sharp with fresh pine. Carl smiles, alert and ready. Sharon, a look of blissful amazement on her face, stretches. Effortlessly, she does a downward dog, one of her yoga moves. Melissa, placing her stone in her zippered pocket, adjusts her white mohair headband.

We pass through knee-high drifts, grinning. Only now, upon landing, does the cold air sting my face. My cheeks feel like glass. My nose doesn't feel like my nose; it's numb. *Strange.* Otherwise, I'm stoked, overheated like I was this afternoon while cross-country skiing.

"The marks, the musta luminae, the Mustelids—are all in sync."

Melissa looks confused. "The Mustelids?"

Carl clarifies: "The badgers."

"Oh, yeah. Forgot my manners. They're not rodents."

Something takes Sharon by surprise. Quickly, she reaches for her ankle. Her thoughts jibe with mine.

"The mark on my ankle feels warm. I think it's keeping my whole body comfortable like some kind of thermostat."

"Yeah," Carl agrees, "you may be right about that. I feel the same."

"I don't know what I am," Melissa confides, "cold, warm, dead, alive? Probably in complete shock." She sighs. "I saw my whole modeling career pass before my eyes."

Carl smiles. He's off in a zone. "Cool landing. Very cool."

I scan the clearing for the badgers. "Would you say we were auto-piloted?"

"Yeah, like I was a fish being reeled in." Carl reaches for Melissa. "And hey, look at this beautiful catch."

Sharon interrupts. "Time to focus. Put the musta luminae safely away. Pockets, pouches, zip them up—whatever works."

Carl salutes. "Yes ma'am."

My excitement moves into fifth gear. "Uh, guys, I'd say we've made our rendezvous! Check it out!"

Silhouetted by moonlight at the height of the ridge, the two badgers appear. From my perspective, they look like stealth bombers with ears. They remain perfectly still as we slowly edge forward. I lead and approach, leaving a safe distance between us. Pausing, I wait for some kind of signal. Instantly something silver shimmers and reflects back at us. At a distance of three yards, I stop short. On their heads are tiny crystalline crowns. A badger king and queen.

Carl continues to stare. "Man, they're … royalty!"

Still in awe, I squint and then acknowledge this. "And to direct us here, to such a remote location—"

"They've got to have a really pressing agenda."

"Whatever it is," Sharon muses, "draws them from the safety of their sett—"

"To us!" Melissa's amber eyes shine. "They actually have crowns!"

"Melissa, ssh!" I watch the badgers move closer as they scan the setting.

Dense woods surround us. When I look up, the moon startles me. There's a faint green tinge around the circumference. By my watch, it's exactly midnight. I look again to make sure. At once, the badgers change course. Cautiously sniffing the air, sensing we are ready, the badgers begin to lead us. They move forward, wait for us to follow. Only then do they continue. They amble a short distance to a jagged rock wall with an overhang. Anxiously, we follow them to a level spot free of snow that looks like a slab of limestone. For whatever reason, they approach Sharon and take their places on either side. Suddenly they make a noise, a kind of chitter. To my astonishment, Sharon nods her head as if she understands. I'm sure of it. They have to be guiding her. Sharon takes her musta lumina and raises it above her head as the greenish beams illuminate a rock wall. The layered wall suddenly opens and retreats sideways.

"A portal!" I'm not sure which of us whispers.

Unfazed, protectively flanked by the badgers, Sharon enters gracefully. Tucking my head, I shadow her, with Carl and Melissa following directly behind. We move between tall rock walls. After a sharp turn, I freeze at the sight. A kind of museum exhibit, an ancient display, looms in front of us; a giant butterfly is etched in stone. I call out and hear my voice echo.

"A petroglyph!" This is a common word at home. "Looks like an ancient carving—and a beautiful butterfly, at that."

"Close," Carl replies. "Hate to sound dorky, But actually, that's a moth. A luna moth, I'd guess. Look, you can tell by the extended downward shape of the wings."

"You have dork in you," Sharon says, "but not much."

Melissa comes to his defense. "I think it's great. Carl is more knowledgeable about nature than any of us."

"Hardly," Carl replies. "Davie knows volumes." He examines the carving closely. "This is pretty accurate." He steps back. "A while back, for the Scouts, I had to present a project comparing butterflies to moths." He points to the finely etched scales. "Wing patterns defend them against predators. In fact, in a hickory or persimmon, they're practically invisible."

"What color are they?" Melissa asks, touching the sandy-colored rock. "Really?"

"Shades of green. Yellow-green, pale blue-green, lime green."

Melissa grabs Carl's arm. "Like … the musta luminae."

"Yes. I suppose so."

We follow the badgers to a narrowing passageway. Fitting through may be a problem. Fortunately, it's just tall and wide enough to scrape though. Carl goes first; Melissa follows him. Oddly, light emanates from her hand. A pale green. So the musta luminae clearly have multiple functions. I test out my hunch. Taking my stone, I raise it above my head. Sharon copies me, then Melissa, then Carl. Suddenly the limestone walls are illuminated. The layers of sedimentary rock become clearer. The meandering cracks and small fissures become more visible.

"Just take it slow," Sharon advises, turning around. She puts her hand on the rock wall for balance and shakes water from her fingers. "Icy cold."

Easily, I peer over her shoulder to a widening space. "We're in luck, Sharon. A cavern."

The going is tight as we edge along another ten feet. Ahead of us, the badgers lead us into an unexpected dome-like arena. It's startling. My legs feel cemented into the ground as I stare at another carving in the rock. A petroglyph, six feet wide, of a familiar and disquieting shape.

"Gee. My ankle is like ... burning." Sharon's voice echoes through the space.

From behind, Melissa's voice is a panicked rasp. "My mark is burning too."

"Here, let me see." Carl puts his hand on the back of her neck. "Oh yeah, that's warm all right." His calm voice drowns out the others. "Stay calm. Something's up."

An annoying sound distracts me—a steady *blip-blip* as water drips from above. I picture melting ice traveling down my spine. But carefully, I approach the second petroglyph without judgment, as Grandpa taught me. I observe the giant paw print, the five knifelike claws. At once, my palm sends a silent shout throughout my body. It's both a calling and a warning, a confirmation and a question. Yes. The badgers are taking a stand. They are taking their rightful place in the animal world. Fulfilling an obligation. How, I wonder, do we fit in?

11

THE CAVERN

The water continues. *Plip, plop.* When I look up again, a large drop hits my eyelid. Not just cold; stunningly iceberg cold. Down the rock wall, melting icicles create a network of vertical lines that descend from ceiling to floor like prison bars. By the green light of the musta luminae, the shadowy designs resemble jointed spider legs.

"Is anyone else creeped out?" Melissa asks, her eyes darting back and forth as she scans the wall.

"Just keep your head down. Watch your feet," Sharon suggests.

Surprisingly, Melissa obeys. We follow the badgers down an eerie corridor. Stalactites hang like giant teeth over our narrow pathway. Sharon stops abruptly. On her heels, I practically fall over her. The badgers have led us to a kind of mural. Facing us at knee level is a slab of limestone maybe nine feet square. As the badgers stand off to the side, I hear a low growl. Alerted, Sharon and I lower our musta luminae very slowly. Carl and Melissa follow our lead. From the four stones, the streaming green light creates an illusion: a three-dimensional hologram. The wall seems to come alive. Instinctively, we all take a step back.

"Whoa, my eyes are playing tricks," Carl says, rubbing his eyes.

Alarmed, Melissa grabs his arm. "Careful! Something's going to jump out."

"Hardly," Sharon says. "It can't hurt us. It's just a carving."

"It's making me dizzy," Melissa insists, "whatever it is."

Carl attempts to assure her, "It's just an illusion. The wall isn't moving."

Sharon turns to me. "What do you make of it, Davie?"

"Looks like a mandala."

"A what?"

"A kind of wheel. Repetitive. Hypnotic. Usually of very intricate design." I move forward and touch it. "This one's a beauty."

"I wonder who made it?" Sharon asks, taking a step closer. "So detailed."

"Good question," I reply. "Sauk tribes had settlements around the Wisconsin River. But that was recent. Like hundreds of years ago. This thing looks—"

"Unbelievably ancient?" Carl moves around, studying the mandala from different angles.

"Exactly. That's what I'm thinking." It's strange. As I absorb the details, I feel the wheel taking control of me. Rays emanate from a giant sun. At the core, a spiral of full moons connect end to end. The design looks like a string of pearls. My mark burns. I sense it; something big is in store. I can feel my pulse quicken, the mark getting hotter, uncomfortable. I press my palms together. No relief. I'm forced to confront the design. The rays aren't lines; they are crescent moons, one after another, linked together as a chain. Consistent, repetitive moon cycles. Endless. Representing the passage of time. Not just today's rush of activities, but a vast timeline going back millions of years. The mandala, I'm convinced, represents our mission.

"My mark … it's heating up," Carl says.

Sharon confirms. "Mine too. My ankle … I feel it."

"Same." Worriedly, Melissa touches the back of her neck.

Stuck in this confined space, I'm experiencing overload. I try to loosen my shoulders. It's impossible. They feel like bricks. The badgers are agitated. Why? I think they want us to decipher this carving. I test this out. I pretend to leave, to move ahead of the badgers. They stop me with throaty growls. When I kneel in front of the mandala, Carl, Sharon, and Melissa copy me without a word. Abruptly, the badgers grow silent. Bathed in green light, the hologram begins to turn like a Ferris wheel. Yes. Reality or illusion—I don't know. But the mandala is spinning. When a very long minute ends, the mandala stops turning.

"Did … did everyone see that?" Carl asks.

"Yeah." Sharon rises slowly in disbelief. "Crazy freaky."

Melissa pops up. "I've got to get out of here. Like now."

"Hold on. There's no going back," I reply. "We have to make it through to the end." She looks as if she's about to cry. "We'll be fine."

Moments before, I faced the hologram as an observer; now, I think I understand. I focus so hard that everything else seems to fade. Without blinking, I watch the mandala until all I see, once again, is a sun. I press my fingers to my temples. I press harder. My brain hurts. I have to process—have to. My knowledge of astronomy whirls, filling my head. By giving us powers, leading us here to the petroglyphs, they're showing us—showing us—that's it! Sweat trickles down my back from the effort. My head clears. The mandala displays the undeniable coordination of forces. Simultaneously, a solar event and a lunar event will take place. It's strangely obvious—maybe not to Sharon, Carl, or Melissa, but to me. A massive fusion of energies. A partnership of sun and moon providing access to immense power. My realization hits me like a board behind the knees. I lean unsteadily against the rock wall.

Sharon's whisper to me is barely audible. "By the way, I noticed distinctive markings on our badger queen. Strange I didn't see it before."

"And …?"

"She has pretty white half-moons," Sharon confides, "one under each eye."

"Not a coincidence," I reply. "Two halves make—"

"A whole," Sharon muses. "A whole moon."

"A *full* moon," I emphasize, "tonight and tomorrow."

"Right." Sharon nods pensively. "So that's our timeline, huh?"

"Our deadline. Yeah."

"I heard that," Carl interrupts. "Man, you two could be detectives. Instead of *Bones*, you could have a show called *Stones*. That wall sure didn't say anything to me."

"I got one thing from that carving," Melissa says. "A stiff neck." She takes off after Sharon. Carl and I walk side by side. The pathway is pebbly but straight and wide. A relief.

"You know, Carl, I think we may be dealing with a heck of a power source. Totally unrivalled."

"Meaning?"

"Tonight or tomorrow night we'll be witnessing a true phenomenon."

"Which is …?"

"A kind of synergy. Moon and sun." I blurt it out. "Lunisolar power!"

Carl looks puzzled and then stares straight ahead. That's okay, though. It's not the first time.

"Uh, bottom-line me," he says.

I hear Melissa calling for us to hurry up, but I pause instead. "Think logically. 'Lunisolar' refers to any joint action of the sun and moon. Their connection, like during an eclipse."

Carl is on it right away. "A lunar eclipse is when the moon is totally dark. The moon's blocked by big fat Earth, so the sun can't reach it."

"Exactly. These occurrences are predictable; they're guaranteed to happen. But what if … what if the unpredictable happens? An event different from anything—anything that came before?"

"You mean," Carl suggests, "an anomaly, a catastrophe, or a miracle happens."

"Kind of. Yeah." I check my watch. "Within the boundary of twenty-four hours."

"Where does sleep fit in?"

"Whenever."

The corridor narrows considerably. The crushing closeness of the rock walls on either side suddenly feels good. Now I get the concept of the snug ThunderShirt I put on nervous dogs to calm them. Not far ahead, Melissa waits for us with her arms crossed.

"Come on, you guys," she scolds. "Suppose we lose the badgers!"

Carl pulls her close. "Not a chance. They need us as much as we need them."

I look down the corridor. My senses seem heightened. The smell of moss. The dampness. The intermittent drip of water. Sharon waves her *musta lumina*. I can't see the badgers, but their crowns reflect the light like tiny beacons. My hand pulses. I trust it. The king and queen, our mysterious sentinels, are alerting us to the imminent danger that lies ahead. I know it.

12

THE PETROGLYPHS

The badgers move like sports cars with flat tires: wide-bodied, low to the ground, uneven gaits. They slow down. Now all that's missing is a sign—"dangerous curves"—as the path snakes to an extreme. Ten feet along, the reliable rock wall on my left disappears. Without warning, we're left perched on a ledge. With an anxious glance, I step back and hug the remaining wall.

"Heads up," I call out. "Literally. Don't look down." The warning is too late for Carl.

"Whoa! Looks like a chasm of ... of unknown depth," he remarks, refusing to use the obvious words, "bottomless pit." Carl adjusts his position to block Melissa's view. "Just stay close to the wall and keep moving," he advises her. "I've got you covered." He grabs Melissa's hand. She doesn't say a word.

Slowly, but as sure-footed as a mule, Sharon edges along behind the badgers. "Be super careful, guys. The limestone may get slippery."

The badgers slow their pace. We shadow them as they move onto a flat, sandy slab of rock. Gradually the tension in my legs starts to ease up. The surface ahead looks broad and secure. But then, like a splash of cold water in the face, a rock breaks away beneath my hand, bounces a few times, and drops into the void. I wait. I don't hear it land. Alarmed, Carl and Melissa put on the brakes behind me. But Sharon proceeds unfazed. I take a gulp of air and follow her onto the limestone platform that's roughly the size of a small boat dock. With a huge exhalation, I stretch my cramped legs. In moments, finally assembled, we take in the astounding view.

An enormous cavern opens before us. Vast. Silent. It is an underground world lit only by the flickering green light of our musta luminae. At once, the badgers begin to make purring sounds both strange and comforting. The craggy cathedral ceiling rises maybe twenty feet in places, forty in others. Suddenly a powerful updraft of air rips an old ski-lift ticket from my jacket, sending it flying. *Whoosh!* As I watch it sail away, my eyes lock onto a striking ice sculpture looming directly above. Knifelike shards point downward. I tap Carl's shoulder and gesture upward. He leans back to get a better view.

Melissa yanks him away. "Are you crazy?" Her amber eyes are giant. "Don't stand under those! If they fall, you'll be cut in half!"

"Hey, then you'd have two Carls," Sharon quips.

Melissa's pretty eyes narrow into a glare. "That's just hilarious."

Carl looks pleased by Melissa's protectiveness. I sure don't blame him. But I have to set things straight. "Carl's life, I'm happy to say, isn't threatened." I explain that the scary-looking stalactites are totally petrified. "They've been there for ages. Nothing falling anytime soon."

"Great," Melissa snorts, "I'm so totally relieved. Merely razor sharp and well attached. No problem." I have to laugh. She's right, in a way. But to me the formations look fascinating. Beautiful, in fact. "They're actually made by water flowing over limestone."

"That's it?" Carl asks.

"Well," I add, "to be more accurate, this happens over a ridiculously long time." I can't remember if it's hundreds, thousands, millions, or billions of years. "Just think of it as a party. Water hangs out with calcium and other friendly minerals."

"You should teach, Davie," Sharon replies.

Carl counts the stalactites and does a double-take. "Five, ten, fifteen, twenty." He pauses. "Does anyone else see it?"

Melissa tugs on his arm. "See what? Come on, Carl, can't we get going?"

"They look pretty typical," I remark, "for stalactites."

"Mira! Check it out!" Carl breaks away, gets down low and looks up.

"Those are claws! Four sets of five." He pauses for a response. "Doesn't that tell you something?"

Sharon tilts her head at various angles. "Gee, Carl. Could be *sets* of claws. Yeah. One for each of us."

Melissa objects. "I say you're all losing it."

Carl shakes his head. "Think so? Look again from my angle."

"Jeez!" Melissa twists her body and then recovers. The expression on her face tells me she's seen enough. "Fine. They're claws." Anxiously, she motions that the badgers are heading forward.

From the landing, we take a steep, descending stone stairway that hugs the rock wall to our left. I imagine we're heading toward the cave floor. If so, I can only wonder how far down we are heading. The descent feels almost hypnotic, with extra attention paid to every step. Luckily the steps are broad, and an outcropping of rock serves as a miraculous banister. Descending, I decide, is way harder than climbing. About thirty feet down, the stairway levels off onto a large circular stone patio that juts out over the cavern. Whatever lies below is concealed by a waist-high stone wall. The badgers wait as we regain our balance. They seem agitated. Their lumbering trot halts. It surprises me how much they resemble tiny bears. I observe their broad heads, long muzzles, prominent noses. Their feet, too, look broad and flat like a bear's. Both badgers now sniff repeatedly, as if sensing some kind of danger. The male presents his canines and makes a snuffling sound. The female badger answers with a kind of bark. Looking directly ahead, maybe a dozen feet away, I feel like I've been transported to a screening room. The wall facing us reminds me of a miniature IMAX theatre—a shiny expanse; a smooth, wide surface of rock. Now showing: another petroglyph.

More startling than the others, this carving is panoramic, extending at least four yards across. It's primitive looking, with very basic shapes. A progression of four hills is symbolized, each hill unique. The first is a rolling hill fully covered with trees represented simply by triangles on sticks; the second hill, a mere scattering of small triangle trees; the third hill, completely barren of trees; and the fourth hill, a jarring sight—an amputation. Clearly, the hilltop is gone, removed—the familiar roundness cleanly cut as if by a chainsaw or, worse, a guillotine. A stark plateau remains. Next to it, as a sad reminder, the hilltop sits like a severed head. This gets to me in a major way. I feel haunted, weak, as though I'm the hill about to fall. I grab onto the ledge as the others fall in beside me. This petroglyph—the alarming sequence, the gradual decline—seems all too real. I feel like a witness to a murder.

"It's like ... like a beheading."

"Yeah, of nature."

I come right to the point. "It's called mountaintop removal."

"No way," Sharon protests, "Do they—do they really do that?"

"Afraid so. It's called hilltop mining."

I shiver and close my eyes. My chest aches as though I'm in mourning. I think of the Baraboo Highlands. Of Sauk Point. I think of the lowlands. Parfrey's Glen. The memories of Terrence, Grandpa's dog—how we used to walk the fields of wildflowers and hide beneath the skirt of hemlocks' branches. I wonder. Someday, that beautiful hideaway could be a sand-mining operation. I take one last look at the petroglyph. If this wall is a prophesy, I wonder what else is coming.

13

THE SHIELD

My shoulders ache. My need for sleep makes me want to curl up on the nearest horizontal slab of rock. Melissa, unusually silent, is dragging. With an intense curiosity, Carl touches every surface within reach. Steady and determined, Sharon stays glued to the badgers even as their pace changes. I feel a jolt. All at once, they both begin an awkward trot uphill, accompanied by staccato shrieks. I can only interpret these sounds as the excitement of nearing an exit. At last I feel a surge of energy as a moonlit opening appears at the top of the rise. We head toward the silver light.

Our tour is not quite over, however. As we catch our breath, one last petroglyph greets us. Facing this illustration, our trusty badger guides instantly transform. Their voices become growls, their posture defensive. Highly agitated by whatever this wall represents, they display the aggression we haven't yet seen—aggression they are famous for. With continual shrieks, they now show sharp teeth and fierce claws not to us but to the carving. I struggle to make sense, to interpret what I see. A giant male figure holds a primitive tree in his mouth. His hands are shaped like shovels. Behind him, three distinctive mounds rise up to form a background.

"Pyramids?" Carl wonders aloud, barely audible over the noise.

"What?" The meaning of this carving is frightfully clear to me.

Melissa groans. "My ears ..."

"Sand!" Sharon exclaims, staying a safe distance from the riled badgers. "Those represent piles of sand." She's nailed it.

Melissa's voice is high-pitched. "And a monster ..."

"In a way." Practically shouting, I offer my best guess. "Some kind of digging machine." I mumble mostly to myself. "Take your pick."

"Yeah," Carl says, coming close enough to hear, "a big-ass machine moving sand."

Abruptly, it quiets down. A major relief. Having clearly expressed themselves, it appears the badgers are satisfied. They pause and stare at me. I stare back and nod, a hopeful attempt to communicate with them. They turn and move rapidly toward the exit. I believe they have faith in me; that I understand this carving; and that I have absorbed the meaning of this wall. I feel elated. The sense of connection between us is strong. Sharon's voice breaks through.

"What takes the place of all that sand?"

I shrug. "Something would have to fill in the spaces ..."

"Like what?" Carl asks. "Maybe nothing. Remember the sinkhole?"

"I suppose anything's possible." Melissa glances at me. "Right?"

"Well, yeah." My thoughts turn to Grandpa: his research, his efforts, his talks at the town hall. "Maybe some kind of pollution. A contaminant." I stop in midthought as the middle of the petroglyph begins to glow.

Backing away, Melissa keeps one eye on the exit. "It's ... copper."

I move closer. "It's ... it's a shield!"

"Whoa. It looks solid," Sharon says. "Solid copper, and very ancient."

Melissa pulls her back. "That's nice. Probably worth a fortune, but it's time to go!"

Sharon holds her ground. "Wait. This is crazy. Just look." She gestures toward a warrior with a belt and knife, standing in profile on the left side of the wall. A female warrior. Sharon moves closer to the shield and raises her hands.

Carl moves to stop her. "What are you doing?"

"I'm taking it." True to her nature, Sharon boldly grasps the copper shield, feeling its weight. She manages to hold it without difficulty. I stare at an empty rectangular space in the rock wall. She faces me squarely, and as she speaks, her green eyes flash.

Obviously I am once again sleep-deprived—but not crazy. I glance over. Carl and Melissa are staring at her too. Sharon appears transformed. I see a queen—confident, regal, assured.

"Go on, Davie. Take it! It's yours—the Shield of Baraboo." Sharon thrusts the copper shield into my hands. I feel the surprising lightness. "You'll need this tomorrow."

"I'll need this?"

"Tomorrow night. Winter solstice. Devil's Lake."

For a moment, I do absolutely nothing. I hold the shield firmly. And it feels right, like a chance reunion with an old friend.

"Winter solstice. Devil's Lake," I repeat.

Carl cuts in and breaks the spell. "We're ice-fishing there, remember? Tomorrow … well, in a few hours." The petroglyphs whirl before my eyes. I try to make connections, but my mind is blank. "Hey, Davie? You okay?" Carl looks concerned.

"Huh?"

"Speaking of strange," Sharon confesses, "I'm feeling kind of …"

Carl reaches out and grabs her before she crumples to the ground. Then he lifts her petite body securely in his arms and hurries toward the exit. The uphill trek doesn't slow him in the least. I grab Melissa's shaking hand and follow. Aware of the situation, the badgers make strange noises—almost like barks—and lead us out of the cavern. Carl turns sideways to navigate the primitive arched doorway. Fabricated from hundreds of tiny stones, the exit appears to have come straight out of a fairytale. I can't help but wonder who made it, and when.

The cold air hits me like a slap. As I balance the shield on the snowy ground, Melissa pulls off my jacket. Carl places Sharon on top of it. She lies flat on the ground, completely motionless. As her sentinels, the badgers stand on either side by her shoulders. Skillfully, Carl moves into action.

"We have to make sure she doesn't go into shock." He checks her breathing, then positions her feet higher than her head. To keep her warm, he removes his jacket, too, and wraps it around her. Melissa kneels beside her sister.

"Sharon!" There's no response. Melissa takes her hand. "Sharon, wake up!"

A wave of anxiety passes through me. I don't understand what's wrong with her. Then slowly, shyly, the badgers cautiously move in closer. They move and halt, move and halt, as if asking permission to approach. Their bristly fur looks thick and warm. For a moment I think Carl is going to stop them. He doesn't. Instinctively the small animals press their dense bodies close to her. A long minute passes. I don't budge. I can hear Melissa breathing quickly. Carl watches intently. Without hesitation, the badgers direct their pinpoints of green light straight from their eyes to Sharon's temples. In a few mere seconds, as though waking from a nap, Sharon sits up and looks around.

Sharon blinks several times. "What's going on?" She looks dazed. "Uh … it's really late, and we've gotta get back home. Gosh, I'm tired."

"Uh, not so fast." Melissa holds up her hands. "Please, let me recap. You called that copper thing the Shield of Baraboo. Then you presented it to Davie."

"What shield?" Sharon looks around dubiously and laughs. "You're making this up."

"Am I?" Melissa points to the shield.

I pick it up from where it's lying in the snow. "It's a beauty."

"I don't remember." Sharon wrinkles her nose. "Did I hit my head or something?"

"Something." I try to explain. "You sounded very sure of yourself— like you were channeling."

"Then you blacked out." Melissa is emphatic. "Rest for a while."

"You had some kind of … episode," Carl explains. "But the badgers— well, they fixed you. It's weird."

"They fixed me?"

"You look fine," I add. "Good color. Same old freckles and pink cheeks."

"Thanks, doc." Sharon stands defiantly, walks around in a circle, and kicks up snow with her boot. "Okay. So I was out for a few seconds. Don't baby me. Really, I'm a hundred percent fine."

Carl checks her out. "What's my name?"

"Bozo."

"She's fine. No problem." Carl flashes a smile as we snap up our jackets. Outside of the mysterious cavern, I'm just starting to feel the cold. It's odd. Carl looks undaunted, as if it's a balmy autumn day on Lake Wisconsin. Makes we wish I could beef up a little. Eat more protein. Lift more weight.

Sharon looks over at the badgers. "Are they staying?"

Carl shrugs. "I doubt it. They'll probably follow us, don't you think?"

"Really," I admit, "I have no idea. But I'm guessing they want us to spread out." I wonder how I'm going to manage the shield. Crossing my arms, I'm able to hold it against my chest. I grip my elbows and squeeze.

Carl calls out instructions. "Make a line, everybody. Same order as in the attic."

I pull up my collar and yank my hat down firmly. My eyes are still adjusting to the silvery brightness outside after being in the greenish light in the cavern. Just then, a lone shooting star arcs across the sky. I picture my chosen warrior, Auriga, driving his chariot through the night as I anticipate the wild ride home. Determined to battle his enemies, to take back what is rightfully his—that is Auriga. He'll get there because he has to. And like him, I'm totally psyched to see what tomorrow brings. I feel a sense of connection so powerful it hurts my chest. I grip the shield even tighter.

Ambling onto a ridge, the badgers send us whirling off with flashes of green laser light. Instantly, like four comets in ski jackets, we spirulate over the moonlit bluffs of Baraboo. The whoosh of air is intense. It seems as though I'm coasting down a crazy mountain on my bike, my hands in my pockets, free as I'll ever be. The sensation of speed makes me want more and more. Like a GPS, I track the locations of my buddies. Then my mind empties.

The round attic windows remain open, awaiting our arrival. The house is one inviting sight. The choreography of the landing is smooth.

Ice crackles. I feel confident and elated as my boots brush the roof and make contact with the sill. Together we close and latch the windows. In sync, we all let out a huge sigh. It's hilarious. My clothes are coated with a fine layer of ice, but I'm no longer chilly. Rather, I feel about to explode with excitement and ready to pass out from hunger. As we remove our outer gear and boots, shards of thin ice fall to the floor like glass. Then, in the dark, we quietly make our way down the wooden staircase to the warm kitchen. By the light of the fridge, Carl pours milk. I chug orange juice and pass out peanut butter crackers. Sharon rips open a bag of ginger cookies,, and Melissa grabs a Diet Coke.

"Are you sure you can handle those calories?" Sharon asks facetiously.

"Funny."

"Don't you want something hot?" Sharon opens a packet of instant apple cider, adds water, and nukes it for sixty seconds.

I head to the den. Everyone follows, carrying drinks and snacks to the fireplace. Thoughtfully, Grandpa and Avery have spread out our sleeping bags. Each is as distinctive as each of our personalities. Mine is dark blue like the night sky; Carl's, green-and-brown camouflage; Sharon's, fluorescent orange; Melissa's, leopard print. I have no doubt we'll all be sleeping in our clothes. Carl hands me dry logs and newspaper, and we rekindle the fire.

"Grandpa and Avery are the best."

"They sure are."

"They probably assumed we were checking out the telescope, and went to bed."

"I hear you," Sharon replies. "I'm about to pass out."

"Please, not again." Melissa throws a small fluorescent orange pillow to her sister.

"Me too." Carl dives into his sleeping bag. I do the same. The flannel lining is like a soft cloud. Melissa moves her leopard extravaganza next to Carl. All I can see of Sharon is her curly hair until she scrunches way down in her sleeping bag and disappears. I'm glad to be in my warm sleeping bag, which is good enough for negative twenty degrees. I think about how we left the attic windows open last night and feel the sting of ecoguilt. I think of words to describe last night's adventure:

"Unbelievable." "Shocking." "Fantastical." "Mind-blowing." I see the cavern. The sometimes beautiful and sometimes grotesque images of the petroglyphs strike me. I search for a word describing both a nightmare and a daydream that becomes real—the petroglyphs, the power of spirulation, the marks, the shield, the mandala. *Phantasmagorical.* Got it. Now I can close my eyes.

Morning arrives—of course, way too soon.

14

PACK RATS

When I hear the clatter of dishes in the kitchen, I wake with a start. My eyes open owl-wide. The ice-fishing trip. The very thought of Devil's Lake has my heart racing. I manage to hide from Grandpa's radar for a few minutes when I hear footsteps approaching. I play possum.

"Davie? Rise and shine!" Grandpa taps my sleeping bag with his foot. I don't budge. "Guess this empty bag needs airing out. Nothing like a chilly breeze to freshen things up. Avery, help me take this thing outside, will ya?"

I hear Avery's uneven steps and his cheerful whistle as he shuffles over. "I'm comin' … darn if my knee isn't stiff as week-old roadkill this mornin'. But hold on, I can manage." Predictably, I'm lifted off the ground, with my sleeping bag swinging like a pendulum.

"Let's heave this old stinker onto the woodpile," Grandpa suggests. "I smell raccoon."

"Yep, could be rabid, ya heh." I let them have their fun dragging me through the mudroom. The zipper scrapes on the floor tiles. The door opens.

"Out with the bad air, in with the good. You ready, Avery?"

I manage to stick my head out. Too late. They toss me onto the snow with a thud. "Okay, okay!" Static electricity has control of the shoulder-length hair that porcupines from my scalp. "I'm up!" Laughing, I wriggle out of my warm cocoon and dart back through the snow in my socks. Avery is holding the door open as I charge in dragging the sleeping bag.

"Kinda chilly for a mornin' jog, ya heh." Avery winks. "Better hurry. The old professor is already in fifth gear."

"Who you callin' old?" Grandpa removes the clothespins from a makeshift clothesline slung across the mudroom. He prepares the pitch. "Why, it's Davie!" He hits me in the belly with a dry pair of socks.

From the living room I hear dramatic groans as my three buddies come to semilife. I hear Sharon's sigh, Melissa's dry humor, and Carl's wishful thinking.

"Huh? No way. It can't be morning." Sharon sits up and looks around. "I don't see sunlight."

Melissa turns facedown. "Just throw me in the van with my lipstick."

"Hey, Melissa, climb in with me; I'll hide you." Carl tries to unzip his sleeping bag, but the zipper gets stuck. "Great timing."

"Beast."

"I call the bathroom first!" With impressive recovery time, Sharon rises in a flash and races down the hall. "This is survival. Never follow behind Melissa!"

Melissa snuggles next to Carl. "My sister is looking lively today. Obviously motivated to fish." She reaches over and unsnags the nylon zipper.

"Thanks."

"Personally, I'd rather be caught." She brushes back her long hair from where it drapes across her face.

"Consider yourself caught." Carl pulls her to his chest. "You're funny. And *muy bonita*." They're moving in for a kiss when I hit Carl with a pillow. Grandpa appears, sounding like the paramilitary.

"Avery has sent me to make the announcement. Breakfast is on the table. You've got ten minutes ta eat and ten more ta hustle those glutes out the door. Let's go, cheddarheads! Over and out."

Melissa scowls. "Way too early to even *think* about eating."

Carl stands and pulls her to her feet. He twirls her in and gets a peck on the cheek. By the way he looks at her, I can see that food isn't the only thing on his mind.

"Breakfast? Never too early for me." He winks as he smooths his dark hair. It's hard not to be envious of those Latino good looks. "Personally, I'm starved. I feel like a bear out of hibernation."

Melissa folds the sleeping bags and lays them on the couch. "Coffee's enough for me."

Grandpa peeks his head in from the kitchen. "I heard that, Melissa. Unacceptable for an angler. You *will* eat something." He raises his spatula for emphasis. "That's an order! It'll be some long mornin' on the ice."

I devour three eggs and three strips of bacon, four biscuits, two helpings of hash browns, a tall orange juice, and two glasses of milk. Still my ribs show above my developing abs. I race to get ready for the day of ice fishing. Since I know the drill by heart, it won't take me but five minutes to pull myself together. Most of the fishing gear we'll need—and plenty that we won't—is piled up in the mudroom, ready to go. I'm hoping I can find the Panfish Popper for Grandpa. Sometimes he hides his favorite lures in odd places and forgets the location. From here on, we are under Grandpa and Avery's supervision. Believe me—their style is unique, a combo of dictatorial and entertaining.

We get our twenty minutes, and then the stopwatch goes off. For starters, using a clipboard and a sharp pencil, Grandpa checks off his supply list like a coach at the play-offs. Like Santa, he checks the list twice. Grandpa calls his efficient method of packing his "protocol." This cracks me up. Even more amusing, he insists on climbing a rickety ladder to load the top of the old van himself, placing everything just so. Carl and I, the obedient elves, make a dozen trips back and forth until the rooftop bin can barely close. When Grandpa steps down, I maneuver the last uncooperative fishing rods into place before slamming the lid shut.

Melissa and Sharon stuff any free interior space with ice-fishing paraphernalia. A plastic box has clippers for cutting lines, needle-nose pliers for removing stubborn hooks, split-shot weights, and ice-fishing floats. There's a compact propane heater to keep us comfortable in the tent, and four stacked five-gallon buckets for seats. Like a general preparing for invasion, Grandpa surveys the van and seems satisfied. Avery gets behind the wheel and hits us with his corny humor.

"Yes sir, we're doggone stuffed to the gills!" I love the way he laughs at his bad puns.

Sharon carries pillows. Melissa runs back for the tall thermos of coffee and a traveling mug. She hesitates by the van as if it's a guillotine. "This is it. Time to squeeze our butts in."

Sharon laughs as she pushes her sister into the van. "Right. As if that microbutt of yours ever had to squeeze in anywhere."

Melissa steps back and smiles impishly. "But hey, on the chance there's no room left, I'm ready to sacrifice and stay behind. Just say the word."

"Fat chance." Scraping ice from the rear window, I notice a surprising new sticker: "We're not your sandbox!" It's perfect. Everyone in Wisconsin needs one of these.

From the driver's seat, Avery sticks his head out. "That'll do, Davie."

I take one last scrape. "Terrific slogan, Avery!" He emits a gruff, disgruntled sound. "Humpff!"

Grandpa calls out, "A real Wisconsin watchdog in the making!"

"Cripes!" Avery complains as I enter the van, "your grandpa stuck it on.'"

"Nonsense, Avery, You'll learn to love it."

"Free advertisin', huh?" Avery chuckles, "I ought'a charge."

Avery's favorite radio station is conservative; naturally, Grandpa John's liberal thinking gets to him from time to time. Listening to them go at it is fun, actually. It's never mean-spirited. It's clear Grandpa is thoroughly enjoying himself.

"Yep, Davie, it's a good slogan, that one. A U of W freshman came up with it for our grassroots environmental awareness campaign. Sand mining's the focus, of course. Imagine that. Brilliant work from one of our own Badgers!"

Badgers. I manage to hit my head on the window.

I protest when Sharon shoves a duffel bag toward me. "Hey, what *is* all this? Give a guy a break. There's no room for my legs."

Sharon shrugs. "That's what happens when Grumpy Pants grows like a weed."

92

I push the duffel bag back toward Sharon. It hardly budges. "What do you have in this thing, anyway? It weighs a ton and a half."

"Since you asked …" Sharon obliges and opens the canvas bag. "Let's see. We have a compass, a very sharp ice pick, one lantern, three flashlights, extra batteries, a box of matches, and … dark chocolate." She reaches forward to pat Grandpa's shoulder. "Way to go, Grandpa!"

Melissa calls from the row behind. "Surely there must be something missing."

Sharon closes the duffel with a crisp smile. "All necessities from Grandpa's master list."

Avery puts the van in gear, backs out of the driveway, and heads down the road. "We've picked up some new-fangled things, your grandpa and me. There was a humdinger of a sale at the end of last season."

"Splurged on a top-o'-the-line new tent." Grandpa nudges Avery.

Avery elbows him back. "Not bad for two tightfisted old farts."

Across from me, Sharon pushes her pillow against the window. She rests her curly head and closes her eyes. "What do you think we'll be catching today?"

"Colds," Melissa calls from the rear.

Grandpa is on it. "Go on and push the ejector button, Avery."

"It's broken again." As he drives, Avery chews on Sharon's question. "Hmm. What will we be catchin'? Well now, different fish will bite at different times o' the day. Some fish like to sleep in." He looks in the rearview mirror.

"Funny, Avery," Melissa calls.

"It's true. There's a rhythm ta their feedin' schedule. Place is important too. For instance, if we're fishin' shallow, walleye or northern pike will show up. What d' you think, Professor?"

"Well, could be some perch, I suppose."

I lean forward. "How big are we talking?"

"Don't rightly know." Avery takes a sharp curve. "But could be some eight-pounders out there if we're lucky."

Grandpa nods. "With those tip-ups twenty feet apart, we'll be ready for 'em."

Melissa's sleepy voice rises from the back row. *"If they come."*

"I heard that!" Grandpa insists. "You mean *when* they come! We'll find us some safe ice, four inches minimum, and cut the holes. Things will be just dandy."

Avery cuts in. "That is, if the horned water snake doesn't grab ya!"

Melissa covers her head with a blanket. Last night has taken a toll on our fashion designer. Carl is asleep; I can hear his breathing behind me. Dreamily, Sharon stares out the window. To the sound of the road, I review last night's escapade: The attic. Our unlikely means of transportation. The green lasers. The varied and creepy cave art. Sharon's frightening fainting spell. The badgers. Our return.

Honestly, I think I'm too tired to be tired. I rest my head anyway on a neck pillow shaped like a crescent moon. I think of the solstice, the shooting star. It stays quiet in the back of the van all the way to Devil's Lake.

15

RESCUE

I open my eyes to watch pink streaks form on the horizon. The only music is the sound of the springs squeaking from one bump to another. We're surrounded by acres of white maple and red oak. My shoulder knocks against the door as the hairpin turns jostle me, and the seat belt tightens across my chest like a straitjacket. A bright yellow sign says, "dangerous curves." The speed limit is now a whopping fifteen miles per hour. Avery downshifts and taps the brakes.

"Hang on!" he announces. "Cripes! This is one devil of a road." He's totally enjoying himself.

Sharon loves it too. "Bring it on! This is some slalom run!"

"Oh, please," Melissa calls out, gripping the armrest. "Glad I skipped breakfast." She speaks even louder: "So glad!"

Avery doesn't hear a thing. "We're comin' up on that steep downhill stretch."

"Take it easy now," Grandpa says, bracing himself.

"Not ta worry. I'm puttin' her into third."

"Oh, great, the blow-by-blow," Melissa says as she lowers her head. "Gee, I don't feel too good."

"What the ..." Suddenly Avery swerves the van to the left and crosses the double yellow line into the oncoming lane. Immediately he cuts back to the right. "Sorry! Had to avoid a mess back there. Some kind of deep gully where the shoulder of the road should be. Didn't wanna land in it!"

Carl glances out the back window. "Wait up! Looks like someone drove off the road back there—lots of muddy skid marks."

"Could well be a car down there," Grandpa remarks, fumbling for his phone. "I'll put in a call to the sheriff."

Avery nods. "All righty. You do that. But we'd best go back, ya heh?"

"Yeah," Carl agrees, "we need to set up some markers or flares."

Avery searches for a place to make a three-pointer. Fortunately there's no one else on the road. He maneuvers quickly and drives back. We find the exact spot without trouble and squeak to a halt.

Grandpa turns around. "Everyone okay back there?"

"I uh … don't think so." Melissa says hesitantly.

"Hurry," Carl says as he helps Melissa squeeze through. "Open the door."

"Done."

Melissa flies down the steps, and doubles over, carsick in the snow. Sharon crawls over me, gets out, and hands her sister a pile of tissues. Carl steps out, but his attention is instantly drawn to the gully down below. He walks to the edge and waves me over. I toss off the snake of a seatbelt and jump down. Carl's instincts are right on. We're at the scene of an accident. A battered SUV, an old maroon Mitsubishi Montero, sits in a sizeable ravine. The two of us maneuver down a brushy slope, sliding on ice and tripping on ruts of frozen mud. Carl pauses at a reasonable distance, maybe ten yards from the wreck. I start to move forward, but he puts his hand out to stop me.

"Best be careful."

"Hope nobody's in there."

He scopes the scene. "Doesn't look like it, does it?"

From what I can see, the vehicle is badly smashed. The fall from the road has turned it completely backward.

"Carl, listen!"

"Yeah, I hear it."

"Sounds like … an animal cry."

"Come on."

Just then I hear Grandpa yell from the ledge. He hollers down to us, cell phone in hand. *No service.* I acknowledge and gesture toward the wreck. I signal for him not to come down. No way he'd ever get back up. Carl and I move slowly around tangled tree stumps and wild pine branches. We approach the site as if it were a large wounded animal—cautiously. The whole site seems to throb with pain. I don't know how, but I feel it. There's glass everywhere. By the looks of it, this battered old model could be one of the very first SUVs. Maybe even from the eighties. There's caked rust where the mounted spare should be.

"Looks like an eighty-nine." Carl knows his cars.

"You think?"

"A real oldie. Liked to have seen it brand-new."

First we hear scratching. A panicky cry is followed by persistent squeals. Whatever it is knows we're here.

I turn to Carl. "It can smell us."

"Definitely you."

"Yeah, right."

The squeals turn to low growls as we lean against the front bumper. Carl grabs the frame of the broken side window and pulls himself along toward the rear. I copy him. To our relief, there's nobody inside. No person, that is. The windshield is destroyed—half of it shattered, the other half entirely gone. Everywhere—on the crushed hood, on the ground, on the dashboard—nickel-size pieces of glass glimmer. Partially covering the rear window, a drape of mud hangs like a brown curtain. The cries continue. We try the handle on the back door. It's jammed. The rear seats lie flat, so we finally gain access through the side door. There they are—two rusty animal cages. Obviously abandoned, they sit in the junk-littered back compartment. I strain to see inside the cages.

"It almost sounds like barking. But not a dog's. What *is* that?" I know before the words leave my lips.

Even blindfolded, Carl can identify most creatures. "A very scared and angry animal." I can tell. He knows too. He's just not saying it.

The larger cage lies on its side, wide open and clearly empty. The other cage is barely covered by a torn piece of black fabric. This one contains our animal. A full-grown hissing badger is pitching a fit. We look at each other, unsure of what to do first.

"Heck of a vocal range, huh?"

"From the sound of it," Carl says, "the poor animal isn't too bad off."

Two sets of claws—short of being bear claws, yet dangerously impressive—lash furiously at the wire. I'm hoping Carl has an idea. I don't think either of us wants to make a costly mistake. Carl unwraps a protein bar and pushes it through the cage. Instantly it's quiet. The badger eats eagerly with its black eyes locked on us.

"Yeah, hungry, aren't you?" While Carl tries to soothe the badger, I run around back. The handle turns freely after a few good whacks with a rock. We use two hefty sticks to maneuver the cage, half-inch by half-inch, toward the rear door. I dash around to the passenger side and grab a floor mat. Now with rubber underneath the rumbling cage, we slowly lower the badger to the ground.

"Davie, does this remind you of something?"

"What?

"Well, the kind of thing my dad was talking about."

"You mean badger baiting?"

"Exactly. A trapped badger is released into a ring, only to be provoked into a vicious fight with dogs. People bet on who will win."

"And the badger, by nature, won't back down."

Carl gestures toward the cage. "Uh … judging by our friend here, that's easy to picture."

Grandpa calls again. I answer that we're coming. On Carl's hunch, I search the back compartment. First I find signs of animal abuse. There's a pile of bloody rags. There are rusty chains. Then I push aside a large, half-empty bag of cheap dog food. I feel around in a crevice. A cigar box has gotten wedged in tightly. I manage to crush the box and yank it out. I hesitate, then open it. It's filled with sets of ten- and twenty-dollar bills held by rubber bands.

"Hey, Carl! There must be a thousand dollars here."

"Blood money," he answers. "Dirty money." With disgust, he takes it and shoves it back into the crevice. Out of sight.

I try to imagine Mr. Marcial's reaction to any of this evidence. He'll totally go ballistic, I have no doubt. "Better wait before we say anything to your dad."

Carl's dark eyes flash fire. "Yeah, but if the police don't look into this, he will." For a second, I picture the inside of that creepy cabin: the hooks, the bloody rags, the chains.

"Yeah, I'd bet on that. But that could be really dangerous, you know."

Carl watches the badger finish his food. "Talk about cruel; these guys just up and split."

"Bunch of lowlifes." While working at the Paw Paw Patch, I've conjured up forms of punishment for people who are cruel to animals. They aren't pretty. The badger's eyes move around. He's looking for more food.

Carl kneels by the crate. "We have to make a decision: bring the badger to the shelter—"

"Or let the badger go."

"It doesn't look injured."

"Why not open the cage and see what happens?" It seems like the best choice to me.

Carl grabs his phone. "Okay. A few pictures first."

"Yeah, Carlito. Good idea. Do the cage, then snap the Mitsubishi." I watch as Carl takes photos from several angles. Reluctantly, he reaches for the cigar box and takes a picture.

"Got it," he says. "Evidence."

Now, very cautiously, I open the latch with a sturdy stick. The badger waits till we both back away. Then, in a dive, the panicked animal scuttles into the deep brush. Carl and I high-five. It's a satisfying moment; that's for sure. At last we clamber up the slope. Grandpa and Avery wait outside, leaning on the van. Good old Avery has been watching us through binoculars that look at least a century old. Melissa and Sharon must have given up on us. I assume they're resting or sleeping inside. I notice the windows are fogged up. Once inside the van, Carl and I share the scenario. We focus on the badger.

Melissa is half asleep. "You guys did the right thing, letting it go." She closes her eyes again.

Sharon flips through Carl's phone. "These photos are unreal. How did anyone live through this?"

"You'd have to ask the badger," Carl answers. "But he—or she—clearly didn't want to stick around."

Minutes later, we pass the sign: "Devil's Lake State Park—five miles ahead." Anticipation takes over as I picture the five-hundred-foot bluffs that tower over Devil's Lake like sorcerers' hands. The place oozes mystery. Bizarre rock formations pop up unexpectedly. Effigy mounds, ancient Native American burial sites, appear as stylized animal shapes. Some sites, I've heard, are geometric in shape. And as the road continues to wind, I recall the spiral in the snow.

As branches shake and powder the windshield, Avery flicks the wipers on and off. The feeling is hypnotic. A squirrel flies from one oak to another, breaking the spell. Up ahead, a park ranger is stationed at the gate—a youngish man with a rusty beard and warm smile. We pull up. Avery opens his window, speaks briefly to the ranger, and picks a convenient parking spot. The restroom nearby is our last opportunity to enjoy modern plumbing for a while. I spot a sign: "Tumbled Rock Trail." Before we unload, Grandpa reports the wreck and gives our contact information. The ranger tips his traditional hat as an acknowledgment and gets right on his walkie-talkie.

We unload the van. Even though we're almost an hour behind schedule, the sight of the empty parking lot tells us we're still the first anglers to arrive. Hastily we load up our two sleds. Weighed down like pack mules, we trudge down to the frozen lake. Though we move at a snail's pace at first, we pick up speed on the downhill. Except for the crunch of our boots, there's a vast comforting silence. It takes some steady trudging, but at last the silvery shoreline comes into view. Melissa, who has been unusually quiet, finally comes to life.

"My mind isn't on ice fishing. Not a surprise, I know." She lets out a huge sigh as she pauses to admire the lake. "My thoughts are on the badger you guys set free. I want to follow it, to see where it goes, to make sure the little creature finds its way home."

"Probably home and happy and not worryin' a bristle about you!" Avery gestures broadly to the horizon. "You won't find a prettier lake. Why, it looks about the same as when I first set eyes on it." He rests his backpack briefly on the ground.

"How long ago was that?" Sharon asks.

"Oh, some fifty years ago. Came here fishin' with my uncle."

"The one that made you eat your vegetables?" Melissa asks.

"Yep, that very same one." He grins.

"Lake's the same," Grandpa says. "But the wide-open spaces aren't as wide open. Animal habitats are disappearing, for one. Black bears are showing up at backyard barbecues."

Avery chuckles. "That's why we'll be havin' our fish fry indoors."

Grandpa grumbles. "Where's your respect for wildlife? I swear, I'm gonna have ta hurt you, Avery."

"Go on 'n' try," Avery replies. "As long as I'm fishin', nothin' but nothin' can bother this Ojibwa."

"I'm tryin' not ta feel like a fool," Grandpa says, "goin' fishin' while the big sand rush is all around us."

"For the life of me, Professor, I can't help but wonder what everyone's rushin' toward."

"Oh, pipe down."

A soft peppermint pink now streaks the surface of the frozen lake. Grandpa and Avery keep talking in the background. Melissa helps Sharon with the small sled. I grab the rope on the larger of the two sleds. Carl picks up a tackle box that has fallen, stuffs it among the other gear, and steadies the load from the rear. From here it's just a short trek to the shoreline. Boulders lie scattered here and there like marbles tossed by the Wisconsin Glacier when it cut through to shape this very spot. There's movement among the larger rocks. I strain to see. There's nothing visible, but I feel it—a presence.

16
ANGLERS

I know my grandpa. The stillness of the lake has charmed him. He hasn't spoken a word all the way down the trail. Now, as we set foot on the shore, a voice calls out a few yards behind us.

"Professor! Is that you?"

"Well, if it isn't Jake Von Rohr!" Grandpa turns to greet the amiable senior who saunters over to shake his hand. A little paunchy, Jake wears a hat with earflaps the same peacock-blue color as his eyes.

"Son of a gun. John Wyatt, it's been a while!" Jake removes his hat and wipes his brow. "Thanks for blazing the trail. I followed in your tracks."

"No charge." Grandpa chuckles and introduces all of us.

"Nice ta meet all of ya." Jake is traveling light; a short fishing rod sticks out from the worn backpack slung over his shoulder. "I sure wondered who beat me to the parking lot!"

Grandpa beams at us. "Well now, you're lookin' at a hardy bunch."

Yeah, if only he knew. This is a cataclysmic understatement when I think of yesterday. Some Saturday. The activities whir like a blender; my brain, a smoothie. I wonder how Sharon, Carl, and Melissa are keeping up. I'd like to clear my head. Sort things out. In other words, I need to fish.

"Enjoyed your talk at the All Things Senior Expo," Jake says. "That was quite a while ago." I'm hoping Grandpa will cut him short. But no.

Grandpa nods. "Yep. Almost a year."

"Really that long?"

"Sure was."

"I'll be darned." Jake looks out over the lake. "Mighty pretty mornin' here."

"Been fishin' at Devil's Lake before?"

"Nope, not till about a month ago." Jack frowns, and his forehead creases. "Been fishin' at Green Lake with my brothers as long as I can remember."

"Green Lake, ya say?" Grandpa nods several times. He knows something, but he's not talking. He has that look where he wrinkles up one side of his face.

Avery cuts in. "Heard Green Lake has some problems. What exactly's goin' on over there?"

Jake rests his elbow in the crook of his arm, his chin in this hand. From his face I can see it isn't good news.

"Ain't the same, I tell ya. Not since they've gone and expanded sand processin' in the county. Minin', they call it. I call it a *blight*."

"That's a good bit east o' here," Grandpa says. "Sure spread fast."

Jake purses his lips and shakes his head as if he's trying to get the worry out. "Tell me about it. It's not just Southwest 'Sconsin anymore. Wherever there's sand, they're diggin' like there's no tomorrow."

"I bet you've got a strange mix of wetlands and landfills," Grandpa says.

"All along Snake Creek Trail. Don't like it." Jake sniffs. "And Green Lake? Deepest lake in Wisconsin next to ugly trenches and dirt roads. Endless trucks and god-awful noise."

"Hate ta hear it," Avery says.

Grandpa stares out over the lake. "Problem is, Jake, money talks big. For now, at least, there's a moratorium on sand minin' in Baraboo."

"Thank goodness for that," Jake replies.

"In Sauk County," Grandpa continues, "the jury's still out; and luckily, there's plenty of vocal opposition."

Avery points to Grandpa. "You're lookin' at the commander, Jake."

"We're workin' on it," Grandpa answers. "Workin' hard."

"Then the situation is in good hands." Jake tips his hat and makes a move to go.

Quickly, Grandpa searches his pocket. "Look, here's my callin' card. Just text me your e-mail address, and we'll keep you posted. Any help you can give, why, it'd be appreciated."

"Will do. Sure will. Thanks, John."

"You're sure welcome to fish with us," Avery says.

Jake beams. "Another time," he replies. "Gonna go it solo today. Get the feel of a new place." He chuckles. "Don't wanna embarrass myself."

I look ahead while hands are being shaken and plot a path around a pinball machine of varying rocks and boulders staggered in the frozen lake. The scent of cedar and pine mix with water smells, making the crisp morning air sweet and froggy. The pale sun is up and rising.

"Just keep an eye open 'round the boulders," Avery advises. "Rocks and logs can be a haven for snakes. Especially pit vipers."

"What kind?" Carl asks.

"Oh, swamp and timber rattlers mostly." Avery kicks a log and watches it roll.

"You're kidding, right?" Melissa stops moving. "Isn't this hibernation time?"

Avery nods. "Yep, mostly."

"Mostly?"

"Avery knows his snakes, all right," Grandpa says. "His extended family has lived around here for some hundreds o' years."

"Think we'll come across a few?" Carl asks, surveying the ground. "That'd be cool."

"Oh, not likely." Grandpa's voice drops. His right eyebrow bends like a shaving brush. "Swamp and timber rattlers are endangered now."

"Oh." Melissa doesn't seem sure if that's a good thing or bad thing.

"Cripes!" Avery exclaims. "We used ta see 'em *all* the time, remember? Goodness, Professor, that was some fifty years ago—when everyone called you Johnny."

"Lord, Avery, a century ago at least."

"Viper eyes, yah heh. Remember that?" For our benefit, I'm sure,

Avery takes his time visualizing. "Those slanted eyes starin' at us from behind our tackle box. That snake had us in its sights."

"Yep," Grandpa replies, "never will forget that." Avery smiles as we slowly walk onto the icy lake edge. He is totally enjoying himself.

"What happened?" Sharon is persistent. She wants an answer. "So, did it strike?"

"No sirree, we just left it alone, and it did us the same favor." Avery puts his arm around Sharon's shoulder. "If they don't feel threatened, most snakes, chances are, will stay put, then go about their business."

Grandpa points and charges forward like the cavalry. We follow, angling to the right. He stops at a favorable place, and we all put on the necessary ice cleats. It's nonnegotiable, just like the no-tennis-shoes rule.

Then Grandpa hands Melissa a tape measure and Carl a cordless drill. "Okay then! My team, Carl and Melissa, come on and take a walk." It isn't long before they've made their way forty feet out. They follow Grandpa, who holds a metal spud bar he taps on the ice in front of him. One of his older tools, the bar has a chisel at one end. If the bar bounces off the ice, he moves on; if it breaks the ice, he moves back. The auger, of course, is more modern and has replaced the bar for making ice holes. It's a neat tool, and I love to use it. Taking measurements of the ice is key. Ice less than six inches thick can be trouble.

At last, Carl waves and gives a thumbs-up. That's our go-ahead to start setting up the tent. Sharon and I ease the sleds onto the ice as Avery directs us.

"Gotta find a place that's just right." Avery wanders around in a circle and then stops. "This'll do just fine. A bit shallow is what we need." He points to the spot, and the brand-new tent comes out of the box. It's impressive and looks high-tech. The vivid blue color nearly knocks me over.

"Okay, Davie." Avery grabs one end of the tent and hands it to me. "Sharon, you come round the middle. We'll spread it out flat. Then it's supposed ta pop up by itself."

Sharon touches the expanding nylon. "Whoa! Very state of the art, Avery." When the tent grows to full size, she starts tying down the window flaps. "This tent's a miracle."

"Bring in the *new*, I say, but keep the *old*." He winks.

I make sure the tent is securely staked to the ice, then I step back and admire the "Command Post," as the box reads. The tent bears a resemblance to a flying saucer. "Great pick, Avery!" I say.

Sharon looks out in the distance. "Grandpa sure is a hoot, isn't he? Look how happy he looks out there on the ice."

"Yeah," I agree. "He retired to fish. But with all of his environmental groups and activities, he's mostly too busy. I think he's involved in every eco group in the state."

"Two reasons," Avery replies as I help him move the heater into place. "One, the professor knows too much. Ask him about the paper industry on the Fox River. The PCBs dumped into protected wetlands. Silica sand particles in the air." Avery pauses. "And two, he cares too darn much."

I lift. The heater isn't as heavy as it looks. "Yeah, the wetlands. You're right, Avery. That's what got him started in the first place."

Sharon nods. "You know Grandpa. He says it all the time. He doesn't want to leave a polluted world behind for us."

"He works his butt off," I say, "probably in his dreams too. I hear Grandpa talk in his sleep sometimes."

Avery chuckles as he adjusts his backpack. "Luckily he doesn't sleepwalk. He'd be handin' out pamphlets in Montana."

Sharon unzips the door flap. "Once a geologist, always a geologist." That's what my mom says.

"Well, protectin' Sauk County ain't an easy job." Avery follows Sharon into the tent. "The wolves are at the door."

I duck in and enter into a world of blue light. I open the interior window flap. "Boy, just look at this beautiful lake."

"Sure is," Avery peeks through. "Now the Le Croix River, that's the total opposite. Cripes, that was some mess."

"What happened there?" Sharon asks, separating the five-gallon buckets. "I had no idea there was so much going on."

"Well," Avery continues, "seems polluted water from a holding pond kept pourin' into the river. Five days' worth. And your grandpa is talkin' about Clark and Trempealeau counties. There's the Panther Creek accident and mudslide."

I pull a folded brochure out of my pocket. "Check this out—picked it up at the ranger's booth."

Sharon reads. "'Wisconsin, one of the most scenic states in America ...'"

I unload the lights from a nylon bag. "How do you want to hang these, Avery?"

"Over here." He points to a couple of hooks by the tent ceiling. "Cripes, pretty soon, the squirrels are gonna pack up and move."

Sharon continues reading. "'... unspoiled farmland, deciduous and coniferous forests, pastoral settings ...'" She stops. "Jeez, maybe this is a work of fiction."

"Yeah. Lose the brochure." I grab it from her. "Let's check out the Command Post instead."

The tent itself is a welcome distraction. It's a total hoot. Like it says on the box, piece of cake. By now it's pretty much put together. All we have to do is hammer in the stakes. I walk to the window and observe Melissa and Carl in the distance. They're preparing the tip-ups. These are kits with flags to indicate when a fish bites. She carries them in a nylon bag over her shoulder. Carl uses an auger to drill a series of holes. Grandpa is holding an orange flag a yard long.

In ten minutes, Carl and Melissa rush into the tent excited and out of breath.

"That wasn't too bad," Melissa confesses. "It was fun. Kind of."

Right behind them, Grandpa walks in and proudly surveys the tent. "Well, I'll be! Do you suppose we went a little overboard, kids? Nope. Never buy the cheap stuff for ice fishin'!"

Avery winks. "Yep, you're lookin' at the bargain of the century! End-of-the-season sale, last year's model, and a floor sample." He puts his arm proudly around Grandpa's shoulder. "Ain't that right, Professor?"

"You bet'cha. Cost 'em money to sell it to us."

"We're in excellent shape," Grandpa announces, unloading the duffel bag. "The ice is five, maybe six inches thick in places."

Carl strings up the lights. "I think we're good to go."

Grandpa pulls out and sorts through his gear. "Glad we got the Frabill Bigfoot!"

"Bigfoot?" Sharon laughs. "Sounds like a mythic monster. A giant duck."

"Hardly," Grandpa answers. "We're talkin' quality equipment, here."

"You'd think Grandpa bought himself a new sports car."

"Well, now, it darn near is. This model has a hardwood base two feet long." Grandpa takes it from Melissa and shows it off. "Nice spool shaft. A bait clip. Figured it'd be best adjustin' the trip setting to *light*."

I grab hold of it. "Why's that?"

"Best for smaller panfish and walleye."

Like a kids in a toy store, Grandpa and Avery are entirely in their element. The tent casts a bluish tint on everything inside, including all of us. It's calming, magical, hypnotic.

"Hey, Davie, let's get it done!" Sharon is on the case. "Take the auger from Grandpa. He's done with it."

Inside the protection of the tent, our job is to cut three ice holes. Avery helps steady the auger, which looks like a giant corkscrew. Using a towel as a cushion, I kneel down and start to drill the first hole while Sharon scoops small pieces of ice and powdery snow from the opening. I have to admit, we're a good team. Our work is surprisingly decent.

Avery offers encouragement as Sharon starts on the second hole. "That's it, just keep going. You're gettin' it. Remember—good, steady pressure and speed. Yep, keep turnin' clockwise—that-a-girl!"

"Whoa!" Sharon exclaims, shedding her jacket. "That took some upper body strength."

Avery seems satisfied. "I'm impressed enough ta let you two finish the third hole by yourselves. Go on, drill away." He unfolds his chair by the first hole. "Remember: control that auger—"

"—Don't let it control you," I say, repeating what I've heard dozens of times.

Avery winks and opens his foldable chair. "Before ya know it, we'll be puttin' those jigs in the water."

The third ice hole isn't our best, but it'll do. Sharon and I place our buckets there and sit down. After sorting through the pile, we pick out short rods and find just the right jigs. A bright yellow one catches my eye.

"Hey, Davie, check out this bright red one." Sharon waves a funky red jig in my face.

"I call that one." Melissa snatches the red jig from Sharon.

Carl grabs two rods, gives one to Melissa, and drags two buckets toward the second ice hole.

Carl bows like a bullfighter. "Choose your bucket, senorita!"

Melissa attempts a curtsy in her fuzzy boots. "Gracias."

"De nada." Carl steadies the white bucket for her, his white teeth flashing over his perfectly square chin.

"Now," Grandpa says, unfolding a light canvas chair next to Avery, "we'll just wait for the walleye and crappie to arrive."

"Livin' large, ya heh. " Avery removes his red wool hunting jacket and rolls up his sleeves. "All we're missin' are the seat warmers!"

Within five minutes, we're all in place and anticipation is high.

Melissa squeals. "Oh my God, a fish!" The wriggling crappie is too small and has to be thrown back. Carl assists her as she stands back nervously and waves. "Uh, so long. Have a nice day!"

It isn't long before the bigger fish start to bite and we're literally jumping off our buckets—except for Melissa, that is, who treats every fish like it's her BFF. A nice kind of rhythm starts happening. Humming along, Grandpa places a shiny, good-sized fish on a bed of ice.

"Mighty nice catch, Professor."

"Well, Avery, keep it goin' now."

It seems we're in luck for a couple of hours, plucking out medium-size fish, throwing back a few. Perch, crappie, walleye. Suddenly, as if kindergarten naptime was announced, the fish refuse to take the bait. Since my stomach is grumbling, I'm totally fine with taking a nice break. Meanwhile, Carl is already reaching for the backpack full of food.

"After lunch," Grandpa offers, "I'll bring out Frabill's Panfish Popper." I'm totally relieved I found it and threw it in the bag at the last minute.

"It sounds edible, Grandpa," Sharon says.

"More like something a headmaster would use on bad kids." Carl turns to me and makes a whipping motion with his fishing rod.

Grandpa reaches for a sandwich. "Watch what you say about my newest rod."

Carl stacks the mugs by the stove and hands out spoons for soup. "Panfish Popper? Isn't that an extinct exotic species of bird?"

Melissa users her spoon as a microphone. "And tonight we must sadly announce the demise of the very last Panfish Popper on the planet."

"Try saying that fast." I finish a ham and cheese sandwich while Grandpa's homemade potato soup bubbles on the Coleman stove. It smells awesome. I grab the pot handle and fill the mugs.

"Remember Dad's campfire stew? Sharon takes a mug and stirs. "It was terrible and good at the same time."

"You mean ex-dad," Melissa replies abruptly. "I wonder, do you think he'll have another family with that Wheatley creature and move far away?"

"Where? Like the Yukon?" Sharon blows on her soup. "I can only hope."

Melissa looks down. "I think Dad and Wheatley went to Mexico for Christmas. Hey, they could be kidnapped by a cartel."

Sharon narrows her eyes. "He never took Mom on vacations like that."

Melissa stirs her soup menacingly. I watch as she rips—no, wrenches—off a hunk of bread.

I reach for the loaf. "Uh, take it easy, cuz. I think you just injured the bread."

"Go ahead, Davie. Arrest me for violence against gluten." Melissa makes an aggressive push pass, handing me the tattered pumpernickel.

Like the true Scout that he is, or was, Carl dives in heroically and changes the subject.

"Um, by the way, getting back to Devil's Lake, I've heard some strange rumors. Can anyone tell me—is the lake really bottomless?"

17

DEVIL'S LAKE

"This lake, bottomless?" Avery scoffs. "Not a word o' truth in it. What d'ya think, Professor?"

"Oh, I'd estimate Devil's Lake ta be about forty, fifty feet in places. If I'm not mistaken, our deepest lake is Green Lake. Over two hundred feet in places. The drive's about an hour from here. A bass fishin' paradise, I tell ya—least it was. Used to head over there on weekends, oh—when I got home from Vietnam. That's when I worked for Badger Mining— before I went to college."

Badger Mining. I drop my empty mug. "I didn't know you worked there." This new information makes my face feel hot. I stretch my long legs, which, from sitting low on the bucket, feel like stilts. I get up and start to pace around. Grandpa reads the question I don't ask: *An environmental activist working for a mining company?*

"That's right. Badger Mining," he repeats. "Short story. I was broke, needed a job badly, and, well … we vets weren't too popular back then."

Avery snorts and slaps his knee. "Nope, Vietnam vets weren't exactly welcomed home. Weren't treated right, no-way, no-how."

Grandpa continues. "That job, mind ya, was the major turnin' point in my life. Workin' there taught me what I needed to know. About myself mostly. What do you think I learned?" He pauses. "I wanted to give to the earth, not take from it."

I turn and put my hand on Grandpa's shoulder. Kiss him on the cheek. He looks surprised, but happy.

0

Avery decides to lighten things up. "I'm ready to dig into some of that pound cake."

Sharon cuts slices and puts napkins under them. "Lemon. Yum."

Melissa, of course, is consistent. "None for me."

Avery's hand shakes a little as he pours coffee from a tall thermos. "They used to call miners *badgers*. Bet ya didn't know that."

I look up uneasily. "No."

"Didn't for sure." Sharon hands me a large piece of cake.

"Miners were *badgers?*" Carl muses. "Because they badgered the earth?"

Melissa approves. "Good one, Carl."

"It's our state history." Grandpa relaxes back in chair. "Good coffee, Avery."

Avery nods. "Well, kids, these were lead miners, ya heh. Big industry last hundred years. They were known ta burrow into the hillsides. Slept there. Lived there while they were on the job."

Grandpa nods. "Just like badgers, our state animal."

Melissa looks confused. "Wait. So are the U of W Badgers named for miners or animals?"

Sharon scoffs. "Does it matter?"

"Sure it does." Melissa turns to Avery. "So?"

"Heck if I know," he answers.

Grandpa smiles. "Google it."

"Later, thanks." Melissa opens a small bag of cut carrots. The loud crunch fills the tent. I'm growing impatient. My foot starts tapping. Nothing is biting. During the lull in our fishing, the subject of mining brings up lots of questions.

"Grandpa," Sharon asks, "what's the effect of mining on, say, animals? Do they get dug up along with their homes?"

"You bet'cha. I imagine that happens." Grandpa pours a little Irish whiskey into his coffee mug from a silver flask. "Minin' is harmful to burrowing animals. Yep, in so many ways."

"Badgers are endangered in Canada," Carl remarks. "My Uncle Leon lives just north of the Wisconsin border. He hunts during season."

I'm curious how siblings could be such polar opposites. "Mr. Marcial—I mean your dad—his brother—hunts?"

"Heck no. My aunt's second husband."

Avery slaps his knee. "Now hear this. Huntin' is natural. It's needed, ya heh. Otherwise, animals would starve."

Sharon objects. "But what Carl said. Animals get endangered too."

"I'm not worryin' over some badgers," Avery answers. "I'm a farmer. To me, they don't do much except dig holes. Nuisance holes."

This is getting interesting. Once a Scout always a Scout. Carl is on the case.

"Hold on a sec, Avery, and back up." Carl widens his legs on the bucket and leans forward. "Okay. This may be hard to believe. But badgers actually play a major role."

"How do you know so much about badgers?"

"Well, I've taken care of several kits at the shelter. One grown badger too. Mean Mr. Mustard." Carl pulls his jig out of the ice hole.

Melissa follows, laying her gear on the floor. "Mustard's not *mean*, by the way. It's from a Beatles song."

Avery sighs. "That's good ta know." He takes the flask from Grandpa. "Go on, Carl. I wanna hear this." Personally, I'm pissed at Avery for dissing badgers.

"Good then." Carl is remarkably patient and polite. "For one," he begins, "badgers control the rodent population. Otherwise, rats, voles, beavers, muskrats, raccoons, rabbits—you name it—would multiply out of control."

Clearly Avery is having fun. "Don'tcha know that's why we have shotguns!" He winks at me with pure mischief in his eyes. Grandpa shuts him down.

"Pipe down, you old cheddarhead. Let the young man talk."

Carl continues. "In winter, I did a lot of camping and hiking. The Scouts taught me to build quinzees, which are snow domes. Unbelievably cool. I'd see lots of animal activity that otherwise would be impossible. I'd watch, record, try not to disturb. I learned how to be invisible."

"Like Harry Potter? The cloak?" Sharon asks.

"Not quite." Carl smiles. "I wish." He takes a breath. "But I've seen badgers kill venomous snakes. It's intense."

"Yep," Grandpa chimes in. "They also help by eating harmful insects. Plenty of those."

"That's right," Carl adds, "and even carrion."

"Dead stuff? Roadkill? Ga-ross!" Melissa makes a face. "Think of badger breath."

"Don't kiss one, then." Sharon brushes crumbs from her hands.

"And why would you?" I turn to smile at Melissa. "You have Carl."

"That's right." Carl pulls off my ski hat and hits me with it.

Grandpa nods in approval. "Fine job, Carl. You know your stuff."

"Thanks, Mr. Wyatt."

"Guess you taught Avery here a thing or two."

"Oh, pipe down," Avery sniffs, pretending to be grumpy. "Nothin' but nothin' is bitin', ya heh. Too much talkin'!"

"The badgers have it," I announce.

"And they still get a few more points," Grandpa replies.

Avery raises his eyebrows. "You don't say."

"I'm afraid this is gonna get your goat, Avery."

"Go ahead." He toasts us with his coffee. "I kin take it."

Grandpa clears his throat. "There's symbiosis."

"What's that?" Melissa asks. "Sounds like a disease."

I cut in. "Nope. It's good. You know, where animals or plants help each other out."

"Davie's right," Grandpa continues. "Badger burrows provide shelter for other species."

"Yeah," I add, "like foxes and coyotes. It's pretty common. They kind of share the sett."

"They don't charge rent?" Melissa takes half of an oatmeal cookie and puts it in front of Carl's lips. He snaps it up.

Playfully, Grandpa snatches the other half from Melissa. "Take this cookie, for instance. If it was too dense, it wouldn't be good. If it was too light, it'd fall apart. Soil is like that too. Which leads to this very important fact: Badgers help in soil development. They aerate the soil. Improve it. Consider them earth's quality control."

"Explain something, Grandpa." Sharon takes a cookie and holds it behind her back. "This is mine. Back off everybody." She stands beside Grandpa's chair. "Now when dirt, sand, or even lead is mined, doesn't it leave a huge hole—a gap in the soil?"

"Absolutely. That's where sand pits come in."

"Those ugly pits."

"Yep."

My concern for the badgers begins to overwhelm my thoughts. It's becoming clearer and clearer why they came to visit.

"That's enough. The fish can't take it," Avery grumbles. "The fish can hear. Just so ya know."

"Maybe the fish are in school," Melissa quips.

I counter. "It's winter break."

"All right. No slackin'! Put those jigs back in that ice hole." Avery has a sly look on his face. "We've got a few tricks for catchin' the bottom feeders, don't we, Professor. Now, the bluegills, panfish and perch—they're all hidin' way down deep."

"Avery's right." Grandpa opens a different tackle box. "On to a new strategy."

At once, by the tent window, Carl lets out a victory yell. "Look! The tip-ups!" Excitedly, he pulls Melissa to get a view. "Beginner's luck! The flags are up. The fish out there, at least, are biting!"

"Let's go!" I almost rip the zipper in my rush to open the door flap. Carl is right on my heels. Reflected off the lake ice, the blinding morning light hits me straight on. No wonder they make the flags orange.

18

SOMETHING FISHY

Carl and I race ahead, practically tripping over each other as a violent gust of wind whirls over us. It's sudden and so powerful we have to crouch to keep from being blown over. When the blast dies down, I reach for the string of my hood and draw it over my hat as we dash for the tip-ups. It's a relief to have my neck covered. The chill on the lake is a surprise after the warmth of the tent. My nose feels completely numb and my cheeks are burning as we approach the first flag. Carl's excitement is contagious. I can always count on his optimism and willingness to follow through.

"This could the big kahuna!" Carl exclaims. "I bet it's a giant walleye!"

Anxious to be part of the action, Avery half hobbles, half gallops toward us as Grandpa guides him toward the raised flags.

"Yes sirree! Let's see what we got here!"

"Slow down before you take a dive, Avery," Grandpa warns. "The fish aren't goin' anywhere."

"Well, darn it, neither am I—not with you pullin' on my arm." Avery breaks away. "Don't be treatin' me like an old lady."

"Fine." Grandpa knowingly shakes his head.

As Carl and I kneel on the ice, from behind we hear Sharon squealing with delight. I glance over and crack up. Melissa is pushing Sharon along in a five-gallon bucket. Sharon's red boots dangle in the air as she slides along in the makeshift sled. They are totally crazed. I'm happy to see them having fun together. It sure is a positive change from their continual verbal duel. My palm starts to tingle, but I'm so intent on our catch I barely pay attention.

"Look out for the big fish!" Melissa yells as the bucket-sled glides toward us. With a harsh scraping noise, the plastic missile stops just in time. Without missing a beat, Melissa grabs her sister's legs and spins her like a carousel.

"Stop! I'm getting dizzy," Sharon cries. "Stop, you monkey."

While they're playing, I notice Carl reaching back over his shoulder. I wonder if he feels the tingling; if he's checking the mark on his back. Suddenly he draws his hand away and instead checks the first tip-up.

"Don't anybody get too excited … holy … wow …" Carl pulls up a good-sized walleye, its unique golden eyes bulging. As he removes our prize from the hook, Carl's grin disappears. The fish isn't moving—isn't struggling at all; it just hangs limply on the line.

"Totally weird, Davie. It isn't … it isn't fighting at all."

"Yeah, something's really wrong!" I examine the fish. The color is off. Faded. As I lean over and touch the scales, I'm uncertain if the fish is even alive.

"Here, let me see that." Grandpa wipes his glasses with a handkerchief. Reluctantly, we pass the fish over to him. I fear what he's going to say.

Avery speaks first. "I don't like the looks o' this." He studies the fish over Grandpa's shoulder. "Woulda been some beauty."

Woulda been. I'm really uncomfortable. The heat of my palm increases. I pull down my hood and remove my hat. I'm starting to sweat. This is very weird. I study Grandpa and Avery. Their faces don't lie. Experienced anglers, they're speechless. A stillness comes over me. In my peripheral vision, I watch them pass the fish back and forth. Grandpa examines it from every angle, as though he's going to operate. Avery pokes and prods very carefully, as if he's dismantling a bomb.

Avery never talks quietly. But he does now. "Had to be alive, right?"

"For sure. When it took the bait, that is."

"But this here fish is good as dead. See the gills?"

"Yep. Just by lookin' I'd say this walleye hasn't been dead long."

Avery shrugs and is done. "A freak thing, is all."

Grandpa, though, isn't ready to write it off. We follow as he walks briskly to the next tip-up like a gunslinger in an old western. I know him; he's determined to find an answer. I'm feeling anxious, and my nose is cold.

Grandpa pulls up the fish, already shaking his head. "Not good. This one is about dead too. Very odd, I tell ya. Walleye are famous for makin' off with bait. Tricksters. They've got spirit—lots of it."

"Don't this beat all!" Avery takes a plastic bag and holds it open.

"The ranger should see this," Carl says, his face registering disgust at the slack, lifeless shapes.

Frowning, Grandpa places the catch in the bag. "Go on, Davie," he says, "take these back to the tent. And check on your cousins, okay?"

"Sure." Reluctantly, I take the bag. "What does it mean?" I look over at Grandpa, but he doesn't respond. I'm guessing he doesn't have an answer.

Meanwhile, the girls are still whooping it up. Not far from the tent, happily unaware, Melissa now sits in the bucket. I feel kind of envious and a little sad as I watch them. Sharon pushes, picks up speed, and slides along with Melissa. It ought to be hilarious to watch, but right now I'm bummed out. My mood won't let me enjoy and laugh. The bag feels heavy—very heavy. Suddenly, like a bookmark in a mystery, the incident is marked. The cover closes, for now at least. The burning in my palm is gone.

"Davie!" my cousins call in unison as the bucket comes to a stop. I ignore them and head toward the tent. I kick a mound of ice. I feel angry in general.

Sharon calls after me. "Grumpy, what's up?" My cousins follow me into the wonderful blueness.

Sharon looks blue all over. "Hey, what'd we catch?"

"Walleye."

"What do walleye look like?" Melissa asks.

"They're nice fish. Dark green backs, golden sides, white underbelly."

"Let me see!" She tries to open the bag.

"Don't."

It's too late. She looks in and jumps back as if she's been bitten.

"Yuck! Those bulging eyes. Scary!"

"They're good-size fish." I shrug and stare off. "But it doesn't matter."

Sharon touches my arm. "Why not?"

"Something's wrong with them."

From my face, she gets it. "Oh. Really wrong."

"Total weirdness.'

Five minutes pass while I define "weird"—from an angler's point of view, that is. Bad news arrives with Grandpa, Avery, and Carl. The sullen faces tell it all. The two remaining tip-ups bear the same results.

Grandpa falls into his chair. "I'm stunned, that's the truth, and deeply concerned."

It's odd to see Carl so dejected. He drops the second plastic bag on the floor next to the other one. "Is it possible—could they have been poisoned?"

There's total silence in the Command Post. Grandpa stares at the ice hole at his feet.

"Now that, Carl," he answers, "I just don't know. Not yet. But for sure we'll find out."

Sharon tilts her head. "Some kind of pollution?"

"Possibly." There's a long pause as Grandpa leans back and crosses his arms. He turns to Avery. "Well, only one thing comes to mind. Those walleye could be somebody's by-catch."

"Yep, that's a thought." I read his face. Avery isn't buying it. "By-catch," he repeats. "Hmm."

"What *is* that?" Melissa is out of the loop. "By-catch? Doesn't sound very ... I don't know ... fresh."

"Exactly." Carl replies, "You got it, Missy."

I fill in with the explanation. "A fish damaged by a hook or trapped in a net and thrown back. That's by-catch."

Carl sits back on a bucket and motions for Melissa to join him. "My dad says every time you touch a fish with your hands you're doing damage."

"Good point, Carl. Your dad's teachin' ya right." Grandpa gets technical. "Fish have protection like the oil on your skin. You bet'cha. Guards the fish from fungus and disease. But if or when these fish are damaged by pollutants in the silt—or chemicals 'n' such—why, bacteria can invade."

Avery scratches his head. "But, here's what don't make sense. 'Ya don't see much sloppy fishin' from the reg'lars on this lake. You agree, Professor?"

"Yep. The local anglers—cripes, I know most of 'em—abide by the rules."

"But what if," Carl asks cautiously, "something toxic has been dumped?"

"Here at Devil's Lake?" Grandpa's face darkens. "Always the possibility, Carl, the way things are goin'."

I rack my brain. "Could be runoff. Maybe an accident, a spill."

"But from where?" Avery asks. "No industry by this lake."

Melissa is direct. "Can't we just call it a day and go home?" Her amber doggie eyes combine with the pleading look. A powerful technique I know so well.

"Those fish are gross," Melissa complains. "They have the creepiest eyes ever."

She's touched a nerve. Grandpa fires back. "Those eyes have a definite purpose."

"Yeah," Sharon quips, "to make Melissa wet her pants!"

"Funny, ha, ha."

Grandpa makes his case. "They're not gross. Those eyes help the walleye see in very dim light, where other fish can't. That advantage makes Mr. Walleye one step ahead of its prey. They can detect vibrations that alert them to danger."

"Smart, tricky fish." Avery snaps his fingers. "They'll take the bait and go home. A sunken boat, a dam—anything threatenin' and they're gone."

"But for some reason," Grandpa says, "their natural alarm system wasn't working."

"I think this is a sign—a sign we shouldn't be fishing at all!" Melissa throws up her arms like she's figured everything out. "What's the purpose anyway?"

"The purpose for fishing?" Avery looks as though he's about to have a stroke. A vein in his forehead bulges.

"Uh, cuz," I relay, "you're treading on thin ice."

"Yeah," Sharon agrees. "Ice as thin as a gluten-free cracker. Better watch it."

"Is that a carnivorous threat?"

Sharon stands her ground. "Heck yes, Miss Alien Life Form."

I try to get control of my laughter, but I can't. Sharon is good.

"Let's see, Missy. We could all be vegetarians—just like you. But, frankly, I don't think eating rice and beans is going to make the world a better place. Maybe beans have feelings too—ever think of that?"

"Oh, stop." Melissa is getting riled. I'm glad. "In fact, yes—a plant-based diet *would* make the world a better place. No fishing, no hunting. Period."

"Hold yer horses." Avery brings it home. "For one, the lake is stocked with fish so we can enjoy the sport o' fishin'. Two, the good Lord gave us rivers 'n' streams, ponds 'n' lakes. Third thing, here in 'Sconsin, we fish, we hunt. It's tradition, ya heh. That's what we do! Always have. Always will."

Melissa maintains an amused, annoying stare. "Point taken. Can we go now?"

Grandpa stands. "We'd best go before you and Avery tackle each other on the ice." He looks at his watch. "It's gettin' on. Yep, let's pack it in. Call it a day."

Avery pulls the whiskey out of his inside pocket. He takes a quick swig and wipes his mouth with his sleeve. "Ta the land o' the free!"

Carl and I pack up the Coleman burner and take down the lights. Everyone gets busy. Sharon and Melissa continue to play. Laughing, they deflate the Command Post like a giant balloon.

Grandpa barks out orders. "Careful with that tent. I'll gather the rod and reel combos. Davie, separate the size-four hooks from the size-six, will ya?"

It's easier taking things down than setting things up; that's for certain. It doesn't take long to organize the expedition. Of course, nothing looks as neat as it was. Things hang and dangle. Avery divides the gear between the two sleds with Grandpa looking over his shoulder.

Avery objects when Grandpa's shadow hovers over him. "Oh, go 'way, you old buzzard, and lemme be."

"Go on. Watch how you pack that sled."

Their conversation stays on fishing right down to the last jig. In the background, I watch as Melissa drapes the Command Post over her like a gown. Grandpa spouts to all of us in general as he preens over his tackle box.

"Now I'll be the first to admit overfishin' has its price. In our state, the big fish are just startin' to come back in rivers and lakes—but they're comin'. That's after maybe ten good years."

"Ten?"

"Yep. Ten."

As we finish our packing, Avery points to the ice holes and warns, "Stay back, kids. We'd best hope the horned water snake isn't plannin' an appearance." He reaches into his pocket. I half expect him to throw a handful of tobacco for protection. Instead he pulls out the nub of a pencil and hands a stick of gum to Melissa.

"What's this?" she laughs.

He winks. "Peace offering. Sugar-free."

I take a last look around. By the jagged rocks on the shoreline, I see a wedge-shaped rock move. I blink. Still moving. That's when I make out the form of an animal, a low-lying wedge. A badger. Then another rock moves. And another, and another—all of them looking in our direction. Of course. The badgers, the lake, the fish—they're connected. Do they want our help, or are they here to help us? Carl and I tell the others we're going to check it out. As we wander toward the badgers, I hear it. A loud cracking sound.

19

THE CRACK

The sound is unmistakable. Instantly, images fill my head. A falling rock smacking the lake's surface. A dead tree finally letting go. A storm-charred oak splitting down the center. Or maybe a wide fissure opening up on the ice.

The cracking sound has my attention. That's for certain. Could it be a warning? A message? My focus darts to the badgers. Carl taps my arm as we scan the unbroken sheet of ice. My eyes continue to the boulders some thirty feet away along the shoreline.

"Some crack." I feel edgy. "That was pretty loud. But I don't see anything weird, do you?"

"Weird? Uh … only badgers out in the daytime," Carl replies. "First, odd for this time of year. Second, odd to see several together like that."

"Yeah. Very odd." My uneasiness increases.

A staccato flash of heat stabs my palm. At the same time, Carl reaches for the mark on his back. He feels it too. My instincts tell me to drop low. I crouch down. Carl does the same. I feel something—movement below the surface. I hesitate and then put my ear to the ice. Beneath me, disturbing vibrations rumble through the ice like a kettle drum. Anxiously, I motion for Carl to listen. He looks at me quizzically. Then he puts his ear to the ice. He doesn't move for maybe thirty seconds. When he finally raises his head, he looks back at me with a puzzled expression.

"Anything?" I ask.

"Yeah. My face is frozen."

He doesn't hear it. This really disturbs me. I check the sky for thunder. No clouds. I listen one more time. Whatever noise I heard—or thought I heard—beneath the ice has stopped. Maybe I'm just overtired.

Another crack. On alert, cool and precise, Carl moves into action. He motions for me to stay put.

"I'm getting an ice pick and an auger," he says. "Be right back." Great. I gather it's for rescue, in case one of us falls through. Not a pretty thought. I watch him go. With his black hair, knees bent, Carl moves gracefully, like a jaguar. He's now back at the packed sled, and Grandpa is talking to him. Carl waits while Avery hands him the ice pick. There's some brief discussion, and then Carl returns with a duffel over his shoulder. He's out of breath. Knowing him, it's more from excitement than from effort. With just a nod, he indicates for me to follow. For balance, Carl takes a wide stance. I copy him. The ice cleats help us dig in. We move only ten yards before Carl faces me.

"I've got the auger to take a measurement. But your grandpa—he's convinced there's nothing to worry about. And according to Avery, evidently, cracks on a frozen lake are normal."

"So we're overreacting." I pause. "Should we check it out anyway?"

"Up to you."

"I've read about windstorms causing good, hard ice to break. Thick ice too." I take a last look around. "Don't see a thing, though."

"Let's not bother. We're going home anyway, right?"

I nod.

Out of the corner of my eyes, I watch Grandpa approach. He's walking as if he's on a downtown sidewalk. He's totally taking the jolt out of our moment of suspense.

"Take it easy," Grandpa calls. "Don't go any farther. No need to measure."

"We did hear quite a crack. Two cracks."

"Nothing to be alarmed about," Grandpa insists. "It's thermodynamics at work, that's all. In the cold like this, hearing a crack doesn't mean much."

"No risk of a fissure?" Carl asks.

"Yeah," I say, "or of Carl falling in?" I give Carl a shove. Partly playful, partly not.

Carl grins. "Someone's frustrated and is taking it out on me. But that's okay. I've got an ice pick, Davie, just in case I need to save myself."

"No need." Grandpa steers us back toward the others. "Won't be needin' that today. Come on."

"I guess that's a good thing, huh?" Carl says.

"Sure. I guess." I'm feeling strangely disappointed. Thwarted, that's it. I was hoping for some suspense. Maybe to put an edge on the flat feeling left by the tip-up situation. I can't help it. I glance one last time at the badgers on the shoreline. I'm sure of it. Some message was meant for us. But now the heat has gone from my hand.

"The signs are good," Grandpa assures us. "Take a look. The ice looks bluish black. Totally normal."

"Sure beats me." I shake my head, half wondering if there's something loose in there. "I thought I heard something strange under the surface."

"Well, it's not unusual, Davie," Grandpa acknowledges. "That's ice for ya. But this here's not bad ice, not honeycombed or anything weird."

"That's true."

Grandpa gives a shrill whistle as we approach and calls everyone together. "Let's clear the ice!"

Avery nods. "I'd say the young anglers have had their fill."

"I'd say the old anglers have too," Grandpa admits. "At least it was a whole lot easier taking things down than putting them up."

Melissa still has the Command Post draped around her.

"Grandpa," Sharon asks, holding the bottom edge like a train, "can she wear this to the Paw Paw fundraiser?"

Grandpa is not happy. "Careful with that tent! Go on. Fold it carefully." He hovers over the girls. Naturally, nothing is packed up quite as neatly as it was. Things hang and dangle. "Too much on that sled, Avery."

"Oh go 'way, lemme be." Playfully, Avery pokes Grandpa in the belly with a short rod. "Back off!"

"Oh, don't go gettin' your tip-ups in an uproar." Grandpa gets serious.

"As to our catch, keep 'em in the bucket of ice. We'll turn the whole darn thing in to the ranger."

"Major bummer," Carl says.

"Yep," Avery sighs, "So much for beer batter and fry day."

No discussion here. I try hard not to imagine our fish, crisp and golden, just sizzling—hot out of the pan.

I look around. Still in goofy mode, Sharon pulls off my hat. She laughs. With a major burst of static electricity, my hair sticks straight out. I pull her by the hood and spin her around. Then I shove my hat on her head. Sharon looks like a traffic cone. Satisfied, we race to drag the sleds safely onto the shore. Sharon wins. I turn one last time, to take a final glance at the boulders. The badgers are still there. But something's different.

"Hey, Carl. Give me your binoculars."

"Sure thing. Here." He unhooks them from this belt and tosses them to me. I take a closer look. Camouflaged, the grayish-brown badgers look like river rocks.

"Hey, Carlito, do you see what I see? I see three. No, four." I hand back the binoculars.

Carl checks. "I think there are more—unless the rocks are moving!" He thrusts the binoculars at me.

I observe again. "You're right. A bunch. A whole group of badgers."

Avery shakes his head doubtfully. He motions for the binoculars. "Lemme see that. Badgers? Not a chance. They'd be down underground."

I wait impatiently until he's had a good, long look.

He sniffs. "Well, don'tcha know! Should be down under, but they're not."

"Why?" Sharon takes the binoculars.

There's no doubt in my mind. "Their setts have been disturbed."

"Maybe Mr. Wiley-fox moved in," Avery says. "It happens."

Sharon pilfers the binoculars and scans the shoreline. "Hold on. Uh … they're looking this way."

Melissa holds her nose. "Well, of course. They smell the stinky fish."

Sharon stops the sled and scowls. "Do badgers even eat fish?"

"Not as a rule." Carl joins her to help push the sled. "Their idea of a high-end meal would be earthworms and the smaller rodents."

"You're making me hungry." Melissa says, joining me. "You push, Davie; I'll pull."

"They're omnivores, actually," Carl explains further. "They'll eat fruit, root vegetables, your mom's favorite tulip bulbs."

Melissa sees the light. "Maybe that's why we had only one red tulip in the fall, out of twelve."

I'm fine with heading home. We start the trek up the trail, turtle-to-the-finish-line style. Personally, I'm fueled by my appetite. It's a hefty walk to the car, so we munch on chocolate protein bars. Unlike during our trip down to the lake, the jinglejangle of the five-gallon buckets breaks the silence. The mysterious crack and the weird vibrations are behind us. When the parking lot finally comes into view, I release the sled and sigh. I'm ready for a power nap. Ignoring my impulse to pass out, I snap to it and move into fifth gear. Destination: home.

We load the van, pile in, and head off to find a restroom in the Visitor Center. Grandpa rolls down his window and flags down the ranger, who is replenishing an empty outdoor bin with a stack of maps.

"Need a map of the winter ski trails?" she offers. She's pretty, with thick braids hanging from the traditional brimmed ranger hat. She's dressed for the weather in a puffy olive-green down jacket and lined boots laced to her knees.

"That you, Maddy?"

"Professor Wyatt!"

"One of my stellar students!"

"Hardly. Not stellar, just eager I guess."

"Found yourself the perfect job, I'd say."

"Well, amazingly it took some apprenticing, but things managed to fall into place. And thanks to you, here I am doing my dream job."

By the looks of this ranger, I'm thinking this could be my dream job too. She has adorable dimples. I'd like to reach out and touch that thick, awesome braid. It's so long and shiny, it's hard to believe it's real. I watch as she hugs Grandpa. I stand by his shoulder, hoping she'll hug me too.

"No way I could have stayed just a visitor here. Well, you know better than anybody, Professor."

Grandpa beams. "I bet the scenery in this park manages to amaze every single day."

"Yes sir, it does."

"Well, Maddy, I'm real proud."

She grins at all of us. "Couldn't have had a better role model."

Grandpa introduces us. "Meet Davie, Sharon, and Melissa, my grandchildren. This is Carl, and buddy Avery here." Avery shakes her hand. I stick my head around and wave like an idiot.

"Listen." Grandpa's serious voice is on. "First time we've met in what—two years, is it?"

"Yep. Two years."

"Well, Maddy, hate to go dumpin' problems your way."

"Professor Wyatt! That's what you prepared me for."

"Need to share a few, well … a few major concerns."

"Go on."

"Well, now, We've been ice fishin'—"

Avery cuts in. "Since sunup."

"Now at first, everything was fine 'n' dandy, right?" Grandpa looks at me. I nod. "Found a good spot. Don't think we were near any currents. Checked the ice. Good depth. Nice catch."

"You did okay, then. Not many on the ice today."

"Well, we did," I say, "for a while."

"That is," Carl adds, "up until we went to check the tip-ups."

"And …"

I hand her the bag of dead fish. "Sorry. Not exactly a present." Grandpa describes our location on the lake. Carl mentions the crack; I describe the weird vibrations. Maddy reaches into her pocket for a pad. She scribbles some notes while she listens intently. Her face doesn't reveal much. Not until I mention the badgers.

"There were several badgers by the boulders."

Maddy looks up abruptly. "You're sure. Badgers."

"Definitely," Carl replies. "We used my binoculars."

"Did they look injured?" Maddy asks. "Her long, dark eyelashes give her a startled look.

I step forward. "To be honest, they looked … kind of lost."

She stops writing and frowns. "For daytime, with people around—that's surprising. They tend to be loners. Yet yours is the second multiple-badger sighting around Devil's Lake."

Maddy takes out her phone. "Thank you all. "We'll be checking this out right away."

Melissa uses the tiniest pencil nub to write out our contact information. Maddy offers her pen.

"That's okay." Melissa continues with the stubby pencil. "This was a special gift"—she glances at Avery—"for going fishing."

"Real shame," Avery says. "We'll be turnin' in all the catch. The professor here says you'll be wantin' to check 'em out."

"Yes, thank you," Maddy replies. "Not everyone would be so conscientious."

Grandpa shrugs. "Sure feel bad for those fish."

"I don't," Avery grumbles in a low voice. He turns aside to me. "They escaped fry day, yah heh."

"Again. I appreciate this. You're doing the right thing. Really." Maddy lifts her phone. "Now get home safe, okay?"

We head to the van and climb in.

"Now it's off to the supermarket," Sharon says. "Kind of crushing."

Maddy's already talking on the phone as we drive up with our catch. Carl and I unload.

"I hope they can figure out what's wrong, Davie," he says. "This is a first, huh?"

I dry my wet hands on my pants. "Sure is, Carlito. And I hope it's a last."

As we head out of the park, Avery shares a story.

"Now, mind ya, last January, I heard somethin' on the news. On Lake Winnebago, it was. Mind ya, not the deepest lake, but the largest lake in 'Sconsin. They had a mighty huge crack. Yes sir, extended way out from shore, three hundred yards maybe. Remember that, Professor?"

"Yep. I sure do. Huge lake, huge crack. Thermodynamics."

"Crack was as wide as half a football field."

"See, we're lucky!" Melissa calls from the backseat.

Avery concentrates on a sharp curve. "Mmm hmm. That's what I'm sayin'."

Most of the way home, it's dead quiet in the van. The last few miles, the general mood improves in the two back rows. We're so overtired that we lose our minds. Suddenly we're laughing and joking about the crack. We have a ridiculous scenario contest to see who can tell the best story.

Sharon is holding her stomach, bent over and gasping for breath. "And the crack is filled with burning lava."

Melissa corrects her. "No, with huge fish-eating maggots."

"Worse," Carl says, "enriched plutonium from a train derailment."

"What train, silly?" Melissa leans into him with all her weight.

"All wrong!" My stomach growls, inspiring me. "The crack is filled with … with all the swiss cheese in Wisconsin."

"And the lava heats it," Sharon adds, "to make a massive cheese fondue!"

When we've calmed down, to top it off, Carl entertains us with facts about hypothermia.

"Oh, stop, Carl," Sharon laughs. "You're crazy; you're making this up."

"Am not. This is for real, okay? So after two minutes in freezing water, the body gets over the initial shock. That's where there's this small window of opportunity to think more clearly and swing your legs up onto solid ice."

"Oops. We missed our window of opportunity," Melissa responds, "but there are other ways to get warm." Carl wraps his arms around her and grins.

"We're stoppin' at the KFC," Avery announces. "It's takeout or starvation."

"Takeout!"

"But not KFC," Melissa protests. "There's nothing for me to eat there. Besides, think of all the poor chickens running down Tower Road without wings. Disgusting."

"You're nuts," Sharon says. "Gotta love my sister."

"How about that diner?" Grandpa suggests. "Can't think of the name."

"Yes!" Melissa exclaims. "Can't-Think-of-the-Name Diner. I'm for that. Please. As long as it isn't fast food."

That does it. We all agree to takeout from the diner whose name nobody can think of. It's practically on the way home too. The plastic bags sit between me and Sharon. It's challenging not to sneak a fry. We both take one a piece. The smell of hot food surrounds me as we pull up the driveway. Surprisingly, my throat tightens. Thoughts of the lake, the badgers, the rocks—they overwhelm me as if I've fallen into an ice hole. I'm stuck, haunted by my last look back.

20
CALL TO ACTION

Grandpa's cell phone rings.

"Yes, this is John Wyatt. Yep, Professor Wyatt, a-huh. Yes sir, we just finished supper ... Sure ... go on ... a-huh ... right. So Maddy gave the samples to ... Good, that's pretty much what I expected. It'll take some time. Yeah, testing an' all—you bet'cha. Please do, absolutely. We'd like to know."

Grandpa listens intently, nodding and shaking his head. His frown deepens as he leans, then half-sits, on the edge of the big stuffed chair in the living room.

"Did I hear you right?" He moves his phone to the other ear and sits down. "Come again? Did what? Well, I'll be. What the ... what kind o' fools are we dealin' with?"

"What's happening?" Sharon dries her hands on a dishtowel and joins us as we gather around.

"Ssh!" I hiss. "Let him finish."

Melissa whispers, "Grandpa ... put on speaker."

"Darn bunch of criminals!" he says. "Yep, I'll get right back to you. Give me ten minutes." He sighs, puts his phone on his belt.

"John?"

When Avery uses "John" instead of "Professor," I look up abruptly.

"What's the deal?"

"Nasty stuff," Grandpa says.

Avery nods. "I'm not surprised."

137

"Yep. The badgers at the lake." Grandpa pauses. "The wreck we found this morning ..."

Carl fills in the blank. "They're connected."

"How?" Sharon asks.

"Hold on, gimme a minute here. I'm tryin' to put this all together." Grandpa sits back on the stuffed chair. He throws his head back and wriggles his neck to loosen the tension. "Gee that's tight." Sharon moves behind him and massages gently.

"Maddy made the call, all right," Grandpa continues, "and it seems two park rangers went pokin' around."

Carl listens intently. "Bet they did some careful exploring by those rocks."

"Sure did, Carl. And bingo." Grandpa snaps his fingers. "The damage they found—the *criminal* activity, mind ya—involves the purposeful destruction of a badger sett. It was dug up. A long section of tunnel—trashed."

"That's crazy!" Sharon says, "Why would anyone do that?"

"A sick kind of entertainment." I feel anger rising. My face is hot.

"Did they find clean tracks?" Carl's motor is running. "Man, I'd like to find them and—"

"No," Avery insists. "Police will handle that for sure. But they did find tracks, Carl; sure did."

"What kind?" Sharon asks.

"Human, badger, and canine." Grandpa answers. "Guess that says it all."

Carl nods. "Badger baiting."

"But that was, like, medieval, right?" Sharon says.

Carl shrugs. "You'd think."

"It's like ... a sport?" Melissa asks.

"A very cruel one." I bite my lip. "And it's about gambling."

"Listen," Grandpa adds. "Besides the tracks, the park rangers uncovered two half-buried shovels." He leans forward. "And get this. A dog's trackin' collar was found at the scene."

At this I start to pace back and forth. I feel frustration at not being able to do something, like, right this minute. "So what you're saying,

Grandpa, is that this business is high-tech and even uglier than we thought."

I look over. Carl's eyes could burn a hole in the wall. Melissa pulls on his sleeve.

"Explain. I'm lost here."

"Well," Carl replies, "some people use tracking equipment on boats. Okay, suppose a curious terrier, following its nature, sniffs for prey. Naturally, the badger will burrow deep underground. The dog goes nose-to-ground, barking like crazy to flush the badger out. But the badger is clever; he's got other exits. So to make a successful hunt, now electronics come into play. What could be easier—right, Davie?"

"Sure," I continue. "The dog's tracking collar goes off, giving the badger's exact location. The poachers simply dig down to the tunnel. The thieves do their dirty work. They finish by stuffing their *prize* in a sack."

"Gee," she says, "that's crazy."

Between the four of us, we give Grandpa the approximate location of the creepy cabin in the woods. Each of us fills in observations and any details that we recall that might make the search easier for police.

"Avery chews on the facts and information. "I'd say, combinin' all the evidence—the location of the cabin, the SUV, the tracks—it's only a matter of time, ya heh."

Grandpa calls the ranger back to fill them in. When he's done, he turns to us and seems satisfied. "They're on it. The park rangers *and* the police. I know it's hard, but try and settle down. I'm tryin' too." Avery pours two more shots of whiskey, a guarantee he and Grandpa will be sitting by the fire for quite a while, talking about the day's events.

Avery puts his feet up on the ottoman. "Bet'cha those poachers might darn well be armed."

Grandpa sips his drink. "First light. That's when they'll nab the bastards."

But my restlessness won't leave. So, naturally, I grab my phone and search www.badgerwatch.com, an amazing website I recently discovered. It doesn't take long before a posting catches my eye.

"Hey, listen to this! Is this a coincidence or what?"

I enlarge the comment from animal activists. Glad that I have everyone's attention, I read it aloud. "'The badger's greatest and only real enemy is man: government, baiters, developers, drivers, the ignorant, and the just plain greedy …'"

As I pass my phone around, the heat of the paw print returns, and Carl catches my eye. He taps his wrist with two fingers. This is our new signal for when the marks are activating. Sharon and Melissa copy the gesture. Clearly it's time to break off by ourselves and head upstairs. I glance quickly back at Grandpa and Avery as I hold the banister. They're settled by the fire, discussing today's catch and the whole tip-up situation.

"Well," Grandpa says, "hope we have answers soon."

"There's a boatload o' questions," Avery replies. "Like ta know what's goin' on at Devil's Lake."

21

HOROSCOPES

As we head for my room, their voices fade into the background. For us, stars are waiting. It's time to show off what my telescope can do. Like a car with all the extras, this baby is loaded. It comes with Sky Tour, which is supremely cool. Filtered through a hand control, an amazing list of celestial objects appear. It's like a guided tour across the sky. Totally user friendly. Sharon, Carl, and Melissa are on my heels as I close the door behind us. We've only had a quick intro. Now wait till they see what it can do.

Maybe my first car will feel as good as this. My very own top-of-the-line Celestron Sky Prodigy is black and a deep cherry red. Typically, Carl is already leafing through the manual as soon as the lights are on.

"Hey, Davie, what's a StarSense hand controller?"

I scramble to demonstrate. "Okay, this mount and optical tube are calibrated at the factory, right? So lucky us. Everything is aligned and automatically stored in the StarSense hand controller.

"Unreal," says Melissa. "Welcome to Astrolab!

Sharon smiles. "Some birthday gift, Davie. This is so neat."

"Hey, get this." Carl reads: "'Databases on Sky Tour include galaxies, nebulae, asterisms, double stars, and globular clusters.'"

Melissa raises an eyebrow. "Globular clusters? Sounds high in calories." She heads over to my computer.

Sharon races over and beats her to the brown vinyl swivel chair.

"Okay if we guest-in, Davie?" Bumping and laughing, my cousins squeeze together on the brown swivel chair.

"Mmm." I pay no attention.

"Hey, Davie, there's a cool astrology site. We're looking up birthdays."

"Mmm."

"Really, listen up. This is so *you*!" Melissa reads slowly and deliberately.

> Fire sign people most often have impulsive natures. They see the world through the mode of intuition. They rely on hunches quite strongly and do not need to be told when to act—they know. More often than not, they experience a sixth sense that guides them along and rarely proves wrong. Indeed, they have more success when they do not think things over too much. Rather, they should follow their first impulses.

Though I don't look over as I look through the lens, this grabs my attention. It sounds ridiculously accurate. Makes we wonder if Melissa isn't making this up as she goes along. She continues.

> The fire sign Sagittarius displays a gentle love of animals despite the symbolism of the hunter. Highly idealistic, this sign values honor above everything. The energy of this fire sign must be put in the service of ethical and high-minded endeavors.

I turn, tilt my head skeptically, and stare at my cousin.

"Really, Davie. Sharon is my witness. It's all here, I swear."

"She swears." Sharon echoes. "No doubt about it, Davie; that *is* your bio."

"Good enough," Melissa adds, "to use on a summer job interview."

"Thanks." I look over. "I like the 'high-minded endeavor' part."

"Personally," Carl continues, "I never thought much about astrology. I know my sign. Period."

"There's a lot to astrology." I finger the controls on the digital camera. "I mean, it's ancient. Think of it as science before modern science. Makes us think in terms of cycles."

"I like that," Sharon says. "It makes sense. Think about it; everything important comes in cycles, right?"

Melissa frowns. "There are some cycles I could personally do without."

"Sorry, Melissa, but you'll have to discuss that with the moon." I point to the digital camera. "In fact, I'll be happy to take some digital moon photos for you. Not a problem."

"Gee, thanks. I'll create a digital album."

"So," Carl asks, "where does the horoscope stuff fit in?"

"Good question," I answer. "The way I see it, each astrological sign is a spoke in this great wheel of the zodiac. Like a bicycle wheel."

Melissa is staring at me like I've got antennae. Either that, or she thinks I'm the world's biggest nerd. "Oh no, not bicycle metaphors."

"Go look, you guys. Check out the poster inside my closet door. Go on! You'll see. The wheel of the zodiac is three hundred sixty degrees. Like the whole sky above us."

Sharon opens my closet door and steps back. "Whoa, he's serious."

I nod but keep looking through the lens. "Well, think about it. Astrology goes way back. It's a mixture of astronomy meeting history meeting psychology. And, of course, all the symbols of astrology spring from constellations." I feel a surge of excitement. The Winter Hexagon is in focus right now. We'll be hearing from our badgers. I know it. Soon. My mark is warm but not burning. I'm biding time, growing more and more impatient for them to contact us. They have to come. They will. I hear the closet door close.

Sharon taps my shoulder. "Remind me not to ask you any more questions.

I make room for Sharon. The Sky Tour is all set. It's crazy. I feel as if I'm introducing a friend. "Meet the Winter Hexagon."

"Oh, wow."

This is exactly what I want to hear. "The Hexagon is technically an asterism with six vertices, or visible stars: Rigel, Aldebaran, Capella, Pollux, Procyon, and Sirius." Anxious to get a look through the lens, Carl hovers. Sharon takes one more look and moves over.

"Okay, what am I looking for?" he asks. I stand by his shoulder like the control tower directing a pilot.

"First look for Betelgeuse, which is part of a triangle in the dead center."

"Uh … got it."

"Good. That makes it easy to find the hexagon."

"Hold on. I think I have it!" Carl counts out loud to six. "Got 'em all."

Melissa shimmies her way in. "Lemme see! Wow, this is … awesome."

"Keep looking," Sharon says, "while I read about *your* birthday, Melissa."

Carl makes room. "Look a little to the left."

"I … I see the triangle!" Melissa exclaims. "The Hexagon! This is very cool."

Sharon squints at the computer. "Okay, Melissa, Miss Autumnal Equinox. Listen up." She reads.

September 21, the first day of fall, brings us the artistic minded. They tend to be quite progressive, tasteful, concerned with aesthetics. This may prevent them, at times, from looking beyond the surface. Very much in tune with the times, they are inevitably attracted to modern architecture and fashion trends. Their ideal occupation allows them to dream up new ideas and see them through.

"That," Sharon announces, "is concentrated Melissa extract."

Carl agrees. "Nothing makes Melissa happier than dreaming up new ideas. Making unusual plans. Thinking outside the box. I'll admit—the stars have a handle on that birthday." He sits at the computer. "Okay now. Ready for yours, Sharon?"

"Sure."

He reads.

June 21: Those born on the summer solstice are obsessed with life. They can be consumed by their favorite desire and activities and must guard against burnout. Be assured they are very intense.

"That was kinda short," Sharon complains.

"That's because you burn out quickly."

"Funny, Melissa."

"There's more." Carl continues.

> People born on this day have a major drive to succeed. They are uncompromising and will surmount whatever obstacles stand in their way. Obsessed by their interests, they are very demanding of themselves and others. Summer solstice people must learn to pace themselves.

Since I attend her ski jump and slalom events, I can vouch for the accuracy of this prediction. She's a daredevil. And I've seen it many times. Her need to shine is greater than her safety. Sharon seems to need to prove herself, and it's never enough. She doesn't hold back, even in rough weather and ski conditions. Sometimes she worries me.

Carl calls out, "Hey, Sharon! Your tarot card popped up on the screen. Out of nowhere."

"My tarot card?"

"Yeah. Number twenty-one in the deck."

"And?"

"The card is *The World*."

"So?"

"Well, there's a woman running—short curly hair—who looks like you. She's holding rods in the air. Looks like Wonder Woman."

"That's Sharon," Melissa says. "Tell me—is her hair on fire?" She laughs.

Now it's my turn at the computer. It feels like we're playing Magic 8 Ball. Carl dashes over to the telescope.

"I've got Capella!" he calls out. While Carl enjoys the telescope, I look up his birthday. March 21 is known as the vernal equinox. My turn to read.

"Carlito. Listen up."

> Those born the first day of spring have a touch of the dreamer, which is outweighed by their practical side.

145

They are born leaders who are courageous and strong-minded. They set their goals high. Count on them to stick to their guns when they believe they are right, even if it demands a fight. Those born on this day of renewal are the optimists of the world.

"That is freaky accurate, Carl," Melissa says.

Carl grins. "I can live with that." Suddenly, with his eyes glued to the telescope, he yells out, "A shooting star!" But it doesn't stop there. "And another! Crazy! Two more."

"Let me look." I shove him aside. "No way! What's the chance? Four shooting stars?" I think of us four spirulating over the bluffs of Baraboo. I consider the strangely accurate birthday horoscopes. Now four shooting stars. Do they, can they possibly, represent the four of us? To my disappointment, the shooting stars vanish from sight before my next blink. They disappear before anyone else can view them. But I've seen them. All at once, my mark burns again. My whole hand pulses as if the badger claws are digging into my skin. I tap my wrist—the signal. Carl, Sharon, and Melissa acknowledge. They all signal back. The same thing is happening to them. That's when I know. I feel the claws.

"Come on. The badgers are waiting outside! Hurry, grab your jackets. Throw on your boots. We've got to get to the attic!"

There's total silence. At first nobody moves. Maybe they think I've lost every single mental marble. Then, as one mind, we all scramble into action. My first thought: the Shield of Baraboo. Like a madman, I dash to my unmade bed, lift my two pillows, and grab the copper shield.

22

COURAGE AND FEAR

As I peer through the attic window, a caravan of dark clouds invades the stretch of silvery sky. The moon plays hide and seek, while from below, an army of eyes reflect back at me. Not only are the king and queen in the foreground, but other badgers are everywhere. All along the border of the woods and scattered between trees I see them, shadows with eyes, backlit by the full moon. The badgers are watching, waiting expectantly. As the words burst out, my own voice sounds unfamiliar. "They're out there!" I'm breathing fast.

"I'm looking." Melissa hurries over. "Show me where."

I point. "They're all around. Look for the white stripes on their faces."

"Oh gosh—pairs of eyes!"

"Whoa! And every eye is on us." Carl runs from window to window. "Looks like an army of badgers."

For an instant, I feel like a terrified actor peeking at the audience from behind the curtain. My heart pounds and aches—partly with stage fright, and partly with fondness for each and every animal out there. Although I'm layered and warmly dressed for the cold attic, I shiver when I see all of those eyes reflecting back at me. We're trusted. We have their precious green stones. It's daunting, this responsibility. Can we help the badgers, these determined guardians? Can we help protect the bluffs of Baraboo?

Our last visit to the attic was a rehearsal compared to this. Anxiously, we hoist ourselves up onto the windowsill and take our places. For a moment, the woods before me blur. I steady myself. Carl, Melissa, and Sharon are all looking at me. I nod. Then, in unison, balancing on the sill, we thrust open the attic windows. My warm breath rises. The air seems to tingle with electricity. Maybe it's my nerves. Maybe it's the mark, a constant reminder of our unfinished business.

Suddenly, from the ground where two tiny crowns shimmer, four green laser beams shoot upward to meet us. I reach behind me to check my backpack, adjusted loosely to contain the shield. I pull down on the nylon straps. They feel secure. One at a time, we tap our wrists, giving the signal that all our marks are activated. I'm totally psyched as we exchange final glances. It's difficult, but I try to contain my feeling of wild joy. At this point, my level of excitement is far off the scales. Melissa's eyes are giant as she gives me a funny little wave. Sharon focuses straight ahead and bends her knees as if she's preparing for a ski jump. Carl takes a wide martial-arts kind of stance.

The king and queen send us off into the night. I see only a glint of their crowns before our powers take over and everything is a kaleidoscope. I feel suddenly weightless, borne like a kite from the window frame. I begin to spirulate, my speed gradually accelerating. Even with my eyes closed, it helps to know my buddies are along with me, all spaced a safe distance apart. My inner GPS is working, thanks to the mark. The pulsing in my palm is steady but not painful. The frosty air wakes me like Grandpa's Road Rage coffee. I'm amazingly alert. The smell of fresh snow and evergreen perfume is magical. But the whirling journey is too short; and too soon, deceleration begins.

I don't mind, though my eyebrows are frozen and so is my chin. At first it's hard to move my lips. Just as well, because I'm speechless when I open my eyes. I discern an arched shape coming into focus. Talk about drama. This is a portal. A landmark. The ancient rock formation beckons like an entrance to the sky itself. This is Devil's Doorway! It's unmistakable. Far below, the platinum lake shines. We land high up on a cliffside. Completely in sync, we are guided smoothly to a makeshift runway. This flat rock slab extends below the sturdy base of the formation. From here Devil's Doorway looms above us like a picture on a travel brochure. My eyes are glued to it as I struggle on the slippery surface.

The oversize moon is a handy spotlight that helps us find each other. We gather, exhilarated.

Sharon gestures as a path appears. Focusing on every step, we follow her determined shadow as she tramps along. We lift our boots deliberately and stomp down for traction. It's easy to admire my cousin; Sharon navigates with skill, finding just the right places to put her feet. A little envious, I find myself mumbling, scolding my big feet for continuing to grow. I glance around. Carl scouts from the rear as we ascend in single file. Tough tangled junipers line the path. Sharp-edged holly bushes clutch at our clothes. Finally we're only yards away, looking directly up at the massive rock sculpture left by the Wisconsin Glacier. I catch the moon slipping behind a charcoal cloud. We've almost made it to the top. I scan the mysterious archway overhead.

Sharon stops abruptly and motions upward. She's too short to reach the top ledge. Carl steps forward, and I give him a boost. With his upper body strength, he scales the rocks to the archway above. Then, using his powerful shoulders and arms, he hoists us up, one by one. The girls go up first, Sharon small and lithe, Melissa tall and streamlined. Finally, with nobody to boost me, I back up and leap while Carl pulls me like a tough, lanky string bean. There's no looking down. Just a few minor skids, and we settle on the craggy uppermost ledge. Staying low, we crawl onto the rocky battlement. Gripping the rock wall behind us, we rise in slow motion. I appreciate Melissa's effort. She forces a half-smile even though her teeth are chattering. Sharon, as graceful and relaxed as a cat, doesn't even blink an eye. Our boots enable us to sidle slowly and steadily to the dead center.

This precipice offers a dreamlike vista hundreds of feet above the lake. Instantly, the badger's choice of setting becomes obvious. The structure of Devil's Doorway offers us a giant access window. We crowd closely together, shoulder-to-shoulder, facing outward. The whoosh of wind becomes a whistle; the whistle, a whine. We're on top of the world. Ready. Where, I wonder anxiously, are our guides?

Sharon reads my mind. "The badgers are near; don't worry."

I take out my shield. "Listen everyone. From here on, keep the musta luminae handy."

The dramatic answer is a blazing streak of lightning that shoots upward from the ground like a platinum blade. I *marvel*. There's no other word. I'm witnessing lightning in reverse. We squeeze together for warmth, for assurance, as this flaming arrow of electrical energy cuts a swath through the air. Instinctively, we flatten ourselves against the rock wall like paste. More flashes. We cover our eyes against the searing, almost painful brightness. When I dare to open mine, even the smallest clouds have evaporated. The sky is perfectly clear and wide open; the stars of the Hexagon are visible. They look remarkable close. Capella is lustrous, as clear as ... clear as ... Suddenly, as my eyes lock onto Auriga, the Charioteer, I'm hit with a realization so stunning I drop to my knees. A panoramic view of the situation pushes away any doubt as I perceive the badgers' plan. Call it a birthday gift from the Winter Hexagon.

This night, Devil's Doorway gives us unobstructed access to the moon at its optimal intensity. *Optimal*. My mind races to anticipate the steps in this wild experiment. Devil's Lake, the battleground, lies down below, a glass plate. The scientist in me struggles and then surfaces to gasp for a breath. Rapidly, I sequence my thoughts, call on my creativity.

"That's it! A lunisolar event. There's logic here somewhere!" Desperately, I blurt this out as Carl, Sharon, and Melissa turn to me like three question marks.

"Logic?" Carl asks. "You mean like cause and effect?"

"Yes," I answer. "Copper shield, collection of energy, redirection of energy as a weapon."

"Where," Melissa asks, "is this weapon?" Her amber eyes look astoundingly vulnerable. Beautiful. Hopeful and yet afraid.

"The weapon will come to me." I say slowly. "Right here, into the shield. Trust me, okay?"

"Which means ...?" For a brief moment, Sharon's voice wanders off. "What do we do right now. I mean ... next. Just tell us."

I say it loud and clear. "We need to *meld* the musta luminae."

"Meld?" Melissa asks. "This isn't Star Trek, Davie."

I snap at her. "Listen, will you?" I'm impatient, a little rude, trying to keep up with my thoughts. "Fusing the power of our four stones should give us the power we need. It's a risk—and, I suppose, a hunch."

"Let Davie lead," Carl says. His dark eyes burn with questions he doesn't ask. He believes in me.

I take a breath. I feel their eyes on me. I'm hoping they'll all trust me to do the right thing.

"Listen guys. When I give the signal, we touch the musta luminae together. If my instincts are right, what remains will be astronomically powerful—one super-stone."

Melissa nods. "You're saying four ... become one?"

"I'm pretty sure. Yes."

"What makes you think that?" Carl asks earnestly.

It's hard to explain, but I try. "Four shooting stars. One universe. They're kind of like us, all heading off in different directions. But for a while, at least, they have the same goal; one goal—to cross the sky, like Auriga."

Carl grins. "So it comes back to the Charioteer."

"Yeah." I smile back. "You got it."

"What about the shield, Davie?" Sharon asks. "How will it function?"

"Well, it's a conductor, right? A go-between."

"Uh ... between what?" Restlessly, Melissa waits for an answer.

"Between us and the sun."

"But the sun isn't out," she objects.

"Actually, that's the beauty of it; the sun doesn't have to be *visible*."

"So," Carl says, "the sun just has to *be* there—to exist."

"Exactly." I try to explain. "The moon and sun will work together. Synergy."

"So the moon really has no light of its own," Sharon says; "it just reflects the sun."

"You got it!" I'm getting worked up. "Indirectly, we'll be mining the sun. The moon will reflect the sun's energy onto my shield—"

"And," Carl says, continuing my thought, "direct it toward—"

At that very moment, it becomes clear.

"Devil's Lake!" Melissa cries. "The rumbling you heard, Davie. Something ... something is coming from beneath the lake!" Her face is a white mask as an explosion of ice echoes along the cliffs.

Carl grabs at his watch. "It's midnight."

"Of course," I whisper to myself. "The solstice, when the sun stops right in its path!" I feel myself tremble with anticipation. *Stops for us.*

There is no more time for words. To activate the shield, I place my palm flat upon the smooth, metallic surface. A blazing sensation of heat pulses through my hand. It's like a tiny shock. With a jolt of fear and surprise, I pull my hand away. The mark, the badger claw, has transferred to the center of the copper shield. My palm returns to normal. Smoke lifts from the surface of the new engraving. The shield is ready, complete. I hear a fierce rumble below me. It's happening. Movement. Now the silent surface of the lake begins a bizarre and terrifying transformation. Like glass shattered in a collision, huge shards of ice spew forth from the center. Crystal knives dart upward and outward in an arc, smashing back down to puncture the silver surface of the lake. Polygons of ice erupt like a volcano. Something is emerging. Something for which there is only one name: *the enemy.*

23
THIRTEENTH MOON

We clutch each other as an immense shadow rises over Devil's Lake. I grip my shield so hard it hurts and thrust it forward. Rising from the depths of the lake, a hideous mustard-colored ooze breaks the ice and expands. The shape resembles a massive water balloon that keeps filling and stretching, filling and stretching, until, shaped like an alien brain, the head billows out. The snakelike hissing quickly becomes a loud *whoosh*.

I hear a gasp from Melissa. "It's coming for us!"

Instantly Carl pulls her back. We flatten ourselves defensively against the frigid rock wall as the inflating head rises fifty feet, then a hundred, a hundred more. Hollow eyes stare from openings in the bloated head. Tentacles wriggle around the neck. I struggle to breathe as sand enters my lungs. I yank my turtleneck over my mouth and nose. Meanwhile, the monster's face extends into a grotesque sneer. When the mouth opens like a faucet under pressure, sandy ooze streams and sprays in every direction. It's hard to see much of anything. My lips are coated with sand, almost glued together. Yet, somehow, but I manage to bark out an order.

"Hurry!" Get the musta luminae ready!"

Turning our backs and grasping for each other, we huddle and thrust the stones into the protected center. As they contact and levitate from our hands, a fusion takes place. As I imagined, the four stones become one. With green, shimmering particles whirling, the stone drops into Melissa's open palm. She locks it securely with both hands.

Like a vacuum, the monster hovers somewhere below, drawing me closer to the ledge. I strain to breathe, as if the air is being sucked from my chest.

"Hunker down," Carl rasps, "and lock arms."

"The sandstorm, it's blinding!" Melissa screams. Claustrophobic, wedged in the center, she starts to panic. "One way or another, we'll be sucked in!"

At last the sand monster is level with us. It's so close I can feel the dreadful pull on my shield. Though Carl and Sharon try to steady her, Melissa crumples to the ground and buries her head in her jacket. Her timing, though, is strangely perfect. That very instant, the raging sandstorm increases in force. I face inward as sharp particles of sand beat against my face. Pivoting in anger, I thrust the copper shield toward the blurring moon. Through the barrage of sand, I aim. I hear a clatter. It's my teeth chattering. Then, suddenly, with a brilliant flash, the lunar target reacts. Our moon. Our solstice moon.

Holding steady with every drop of strength, I feel the shield vibrate in my hands. The copper is working, absorbing power. Lunisolar power enters the perfect metal. I feel a sudden stab of fear. I mustn't drop the shield. My heart races. Solar power—via the moon. My vision becomes reality as pelting streaks of light beam forth from the lunar surface. Dazzling golden beams shoot toward Devil's Doorway. With almost unbearable intensity, energy penetrates and continues to enter my shield.

Laden with power, the shield becomes much heavier. I grunt under the weight. Fear hits me again. I imagine falling. Seeing me at the rock edge, Carl locks his arms around my waist to support me.

Back in balance, I change targets. I move my shield from the moon directly to the face of the sand monster. My arms ache terribly. I see blood trickle down Carl's forehead as sharp particles stab at him. He grimaces while together we focus our copper weapon. Sharon crouches to steady Carl. Melissa reaches to support Sharon. We're in control, taking aim at the monstrous head, when a venomous blow strikes. A wall of wet sand hurls me back against the rock wall. I lose the shield. My hand smashes into stone. Carl lands next to me, coughing sand. Sharon groans as she's tossed on top of us like a ragdoll. She rolls to my left, motionless. Then I feel my heart leap.

Melissa grabs the shield. I watch in awe as she stands tall and faces the creature.

"Sand brain, Take that!"

Harsh white beams shoot outward. My nose, mouth, and ears cloud with sand. I can barely breathe when I hear the strike. Melissa hits the monster dead on. I'm so mesmerized by Melissa's fearless face that the crashing of metal on stone doesn't register. Not right away. Only when a bubble of green light encases all of us do I realize the shield of Baraboo is gone. I stare in awe as Melissa lifts the musta lumina, wrapping us in a protective shell. I spit sand from my mouth. Although the rock wall reverberates, I feel no heat, no more lashings of sand. The air begins to clear. Carl sits up and wipes sand from his face. Sharon stirs and rests on her elbow. Melissa holds the green stone, looking remarkably like a goddess. Every strand of her flowing hair is coated with golden sand.

The moment is short-lived. All at once, through the green bubble we view an alarming sight. A hideous tentacle slowly stretches toward us, trying to penetrate our green cocoon. It lashes. We freeze. It lashes again. Then, in answer, a shocking blast of lightning rises from far below. It rises from the earth itself, instantly demolishing the last of the sand creature. The blast of electrical energy turns the hollow eyes from black to white powder. The threatening mouth dissolves. The sandy ooze melts. Stray airborne particles liquefy, then quickly evaporate into a giant cloud. This translucent vapor rises, dispersing upward as the moon slowly becomes visible again. And now, as Melissa holds the musta lumina, its green protective haze reenters the stone like a genie in a magic lamp. One of my knuckles is scraped raw. Otherwise, I'd think this is some crazy dream. Carl rubs his hands through his thick black curls. I tap Sharon. She sits up and exhales with a mixture of relief and wonder. I notice a bluish bruise on her cheek. Melissa sits cross-legged, the musta lumina resting in her hands. She studies it warily.

"What next?" she says in a stage whisper.

First I see just the glow of their crowns. Barely visible from the giant boulders above us, the silhouettes of the badger king and queen appear against a lilac sky. Just moments ago, they were directing bolts

155

of lightning from the ground below. Now, quite remarkably, they are situated at the highest point in Devil's Doorway.

"Look, guys!" I motion to the others as I get on all fours and stretch my neck. "All the way to the top, far to the left!" The badgers. The Mustelids. The royal ones.

Carl is pragmatic. "I hope we helped them fulfill their mission."

"Yeah," Sharon says, "now that the enemy is gone ..."

"At least for now." Our heads all turn to Melissa. Of course, she's right. Who knows for sure.

"I wonder if we'll ever see them again." Sadness comes over me. The solidarity I feel toward these small but determined animals makes my chest ache. I hold back tears as I recall something Grandpa told me: *"Let wild be wild."*

I swallow hard like I'm holding a tennis ball in my throat. I don't know how long we all remain motionless. I don't look at my watch. Devil's Doorway arches above as I rest my head back against the ancient stone pillar. Carl leans back on the pillar across from me. A calmness takes over as I breathe. I watch the stars twinkle as the air clears. The sight of the Winter Hexagon reassures me. Gradually the lake reappears, a newly polished silver plate. From the smog of sand, the solstice moon grows from a pinpoint into fullness. There's more.

Exhausted, lumped together, we nod off. When a pink dawn dabs the sky, Sharon is first to open her eyes.

"Wake up!" she exclaims. "Wake up!"

My eyelids go staccato. There's a strange fluttering inside the portal. "Holy ..."

"It's a luna!" Carl looks certain.

Melissa puts up her hand. "Don't move. The musta lumina—it's gone."

"It's not gone," Sharon answers. "It right in front of us."

"The moth!"

"Exactly."

A pair of upper wings and two elongated bottom wings flutter before us.

"Whoa, it looks exactly like the petroglyph!" Carl stands, but Melissa reaches over and pulls him back down.

"Don't disturb it." The wings are unique, unlike those of any moth I've ever seen. In the gentle light they display a delicate light green color. The numerous scales look like tiny panels of stained glass.

"Oh!" Melissa cries out as the moth lingers by her face. I count four circles before the magnificent luna flies up and out of Devil's Doorway. The sky is growing lighter, the stars fading except for Capella. A sense of protection wraps around me like a blanket. Yeah. The Winter Hexagon is keeping us in its sights. When my eyes refocus, the badgers are gone.

"I didn't even notice," Carl says. "When did they go?"

Sharon shrugs vaguely. "Maybe they left with the moth."

"Or," Carl suggests, "they went home to kick out the fox."

"What fox?" Melissa yawns.

I stand. "Could already be nice and cozy in their sett."

"A great idea, Davie. Copy that." Carl is already finding his footing. We start to rally. Melissa brushes sand and dirt from her white jacket.

"Was all this supposed to be a warning?"

Sharon ponders. "I'd say more like a major wake-up call."

"For Wisconsin, or for the world in general?" Carl asks.

I nod. "That could be quite a phone bill."

Carl motions us over. "Okay, two words: 'home' and 'sleep.'"

"That's three," Melissa says. "And by the way, how are we getting home?"

"That's right." It dawns on me. "My mark is gone. And the musta lumina is—"

"A Lepidoptera." Carl smiles and clarifies. "A moth."

"Davie," Melissa asks, "you expect the badgers will come back, right?"

Sharon answers first. "Of course they will."

"Uh, hello!" Melissa objects. "'Cause if they don't, we have a problem."

Carl shrugs and starts down first. "One step at a time."

Melissa follows Carl. I gesture for Sharon to go ahead of me. I want to take one last look at Devil's Lake. It's still and silent. Though I haven't said it out loud, I wonder if it will stay that way. Is the battle over for good? My hands feel empty without the shield. I'm wondering where it landed, or if it landed at all. Maybe it disintegrated. I'll probably never know. My mind starts to wander. In three days, my parents will be home. Mr. Marcial has promised to open the shelter on Christmas Eve for a blessing of the animals. Bear, the wide-open Jack Russell, and Darla, the dainty, high-jumping mutt, will come home with me. A "forever home," we call it at the Paw Paw Patch.

I snap back to the present, pick up the rear, and head down the sloping rock. At the base, we gather at a small sign: Devil's Doorway Trail. Luckily this is an asphalt trail. From here the varied evergreens obscure any view except that of my boots and the short path ahead. We stop in our tracks at a spectacular drop-off of several hundred feet. A sign for Pothole Trail appears nearby. There's no way. I've heard of this one. Of course, the hiking trails aren't maintained in winter. And one look at the treacherous stone steps and their seemingly endless descent makes it clear; we're not going anywhere—at least by foot. Personally, my transmission is wearing down. I bite my lip and smile to myself. I'm actually too tired to be tired.

"'Pothole Trail,'" Sharon reads.

"That's an understatement." Melissa peers at the incline. "What should we do?"

Carl frowns. "We're kind of stuck."

"Let's hope the badgers are still around." The words are barely out of my mouth when I sense the familiar heat in my palm. I feel a rush of relief. The mark is back. I'll be able to navigate home. Anticipation gives me a kick of energy. Soon we come to an extravagant spruce with branches that hang in graceful curves like the arms of a dancer. I look at my buddies. This looks like a logical meeting place. My palm tingles. They look my way and give the signal. They feel it too. The badgers are near. I glance around, not just with hopes of spirulating home. I want more. I want desperately to maintain a connection with the badgers. For Wisconsin. For the earth. I want to play a part; to act. I look up at streaks of blue pushing away the pink sky. We can't let our enthusiasm fade. I make an emphatic announcement.

"I am that tree!"

"Do what?" Carl eyes me with a touch of concern. "You okay?"

I stretch my arms wide. "Come on. Be spontaneous."

Sharon copies me. "No obstacles in our way."

"Oh gee," Melissa responds, "poetry at dawn. Someone, please help me."

Carl puts his arms around her and squeezes. Then he takes her hands in his and reaches them out like a sculptor. He mirrors her, and his voice echoes precisely what I'm thinking.

"Right," he says, "make the impossible possible."

We all twirl around and around until we're insanely dizzy. When Carl dives to the ground, we follow. Together we make snow angels, flapping our arms and legs like crazed penguins. I keep it up until I can't move anymore. I stare up at the sky through green lace.

Suddenly we're bathed in that special green light. My instincts were right. The badgers stand beneath the spruce, close to the trunk. I feel a renewed confidence in the mark on my hand. I want it to be permanent. I can only hope. It's hard to describe the smell of snow, the freshness of morning in Wisconsin. Everything seems new. I breathe in a kind of hope. With the badgers guiding us, we're about to head home. The winter solstice has delivered the best birthday gift of all: empowerment. The battle, the winding journey, the thrilling adventure. Crazy. I feel strong like Carl, only buff on the inside. So Avery's stories have a point after all. Maybe courage and fear are one—the two sides of a coin, the two sides of a shield.

On the bluffs of Baraboo, nocturnal animals are taking shelter. Right now, the park rangers and police are doing their job at a scary, broken-down cabin. Poachers will be caught, animals freed from a terrible fate. Again, as before, I feel the words on my lips, a whisper in my ear. Grandpa's voice. "*Let wild be wild, son.*" In about an hour, in his flannel bathrobe, Grandpa will pour coffee into a mug that reads, "frack no!" Avery will complain that the Road Rage coffee is too strong. Everything will seem normal. A comforting kind of ordinary.

But after tonight, after the battle, nothing for me—and probably for Sharon, Carl, and Melissa—will be the same ever again. We'll find a way to act, to protest, to speak out—yeah, to badger—until we set things right for the earth. Grandpa can teach us. Avery can drive us. Together with friends at school and at the Paw Paw Patch, we'll find ways to make people aware. The mission will continue.

We whirl homeward. The attic windows will be open, waiting. The sun is an egg yolk. I think of scrambled eggs, oatmeal, and pancakes piled as high as the cliffs at Devil's Lake. I'm crazy hungry. The four of us, if we're lucky, will be home before anyone knows we're gone.

EPILOGUE
THE FUTURE

First I hear barks in two distinct octaves, then the scrape of toenails on the wood floor as Bear dashes and Darla dives over furniture to the front door. No sneaking around here. My newly adopted canines are overenthusiastic about visitors. Sure enough, there's a loud knock at the front door. I'm puzzled. It's a little too early for UPS to be delivering the special moon filter for my Celestron.

"I'm comin' Davie!" Grandpa calls. "Let the dogs out back, will ya?"

When I open the mudroom door, the dogs regroup and bound happily into the newly fenced-in backyard. They redirect their barking as a squirrel teases them from a high oak branch. Satisfied, I return and open the front door. Facing me, blocking the backdrop of white sunrise, stands a man in work clothes. His pants have a nice crease, but they're not the standard UPS brown. He isn't carrying a cardboard box in his hands. Too bad. Maybe the moon filter will come later today. Instead he's standing with a clipboard and a half-smile. I can see right away he isn't a telephone lineman or here to read some meter. Judging by his sturdy overalls and jacket, he plans to work out in the bitter cold all day long. Maybe longer. He wears a hard hat over a wool cap and has a weird-looking gas mask slung over his shoulder on a strap. The sand-colored work boots have metal reinforcements in the toe. Some serious black work gloves too. In fact, I'm awed by all the belted gear hanging off his body. I have a strange, sinking feeling. Obviously he isn't here to piddle around.

"You're staring at my respirator," he says. "Top o' the line. When you're dealing with quartzite sand, can't be too cautious. Silica dust."

I note the goggles pushed up on the narrow bit of space left on his forehead. His bright blue eyes look red around the edges. I grip the doorknob tightly. It's clear a sand-mining operation is about to get underway. Right here? Maybe he's looking for directions. Either way, it can't be good. Footsteps behind me. Grandpa stands beside me as the winter light sets the man's face in shadow. Cupping my hand over my eyes, I make out tons of heavy machinery in the background. Several large trucks with open containers are parked out by the curb. A red dump truck. A green dump truck with giant hoses. An orange bulldozer is already parked in our driveway. A yellow-orange vehicle is the standout. I scan the equipment with a feeling of dread. These are trucks I played with as a kid. Trucks I collected and still have in the back of my closet. Only, these engines are running. Exhaust filters toward us in the cold air.

The man lowers the clipboard as a thick pile of papers flutters in the breeze.

The storm door opens and closes. The man barely enters the foyer. Grandpa stands like a roadblock, crossing his arms, as wary as a fox. Count on it. The workman won't be in the doorway long. In one glance, Grandpa takes it all in.

"Hope you're plannin' on headin' back where you came from."

"No sir. I have a work order here."

"Sure looks like sand-minin' equipment to me. You're in the wrong place, fella,"

I wonder if the guy will turn and leave. I'm beginning to doubt it. The half-smile disappears and his lips press together as he squares his shoulders. A jumble of words pass between the man and Grandpa. I hear two words repeated over and over: "Mining rights." Grandpa adjusts his glasses.

"Frac-sand-mining rights?" He maintains his guard-dog stance. "Best take that thing outta my face!" He pushes the clipboard away.

"Beggin' your pardon, we're gonna do our job whether you sign this or not."

Their voices rise steadily in volume. I don't like anything I'm hearing.

The man waves his papers and insists he has some kind of deed that gives his company permission to dig.

"Now, let me get this right," Grandpa says. "You're sayin' you have the legal right of way—to what? To mine around and under my property? You're tellin' me some joker sold your company the minin' rights to my land, my soil, a hundred or so years ago?"

"That's right."

Avery joins us. He talks his way over to the front door. "Well then, Mister, I'd say someone sold you a bill o' goods!" He looks down and points at the man's feet. "Mighty fine boots ya got, though. I could use a pair o' those for the farm. Bet'cha a bull moose could tap-dance on those. Ya wouldn't feel a thing."

The man looks back and forth between Grandpa and Avery. "Uh … it's all here in black-and-white, sir. Sirs."

"Don't you 'sir' me." Grandpa lowers his voice. "You're gonna replace my pretty hillside with what—a hundred-foot pit? No thank you. And pump how much water—fourteen hundred gallons per minute, is it?" Grandpa shakes his head. "Over my dead body!"

There's a long pause. A kind of stalemate.

"Fact is," the man says, "we're all set out there and ready to begin."

Grandpa pushes the door and holds it open. "Now I'm gonna ask you nicely to get off my property."

The man shrugs, turns, and walks back toward his truck.

Avery sighs. "If that don't beat all." With the remote in hand, he shuffles over and turns up the television. A local news anchor is reporting on location from La Crosse, a few counties over. I can't say the news is unbelievable, but still—it's shocking. I walk over and stare at the screen. The attractive female reporter holds a microphone and looks over her shoulder at a road clogged with honking cars, vans, and trucks. There's obviously a huge backup. Nothing seems to be moving. So Grandpa can hear, Avery turns up the volume until it's blaring.

"Indeed, huge evacuation efforts are in progress, and thousands have been forced to abandon their homes here in southwestern Wisconsin. One entire county bordering the Mississippi River has no viable drinking water, owing to a major breach in a containment pond. And there's more. It seems the effects of sand mining are taking their toll exactly as some scientists predicted. Polyacrylamides—chemicals that may affect the nervous system or possibly lead to cancer—have been identified in the water system. Sources say the frac-sand industry has the upper hand—or, indeed, has won the match. Just yesterday, however, New York State governor Cuomo issued an all-out ban on fracking in his state. The question in everyone's mind right now is, can things get worse for Wisconsin? What will the DNR, the Department of Natural Resources, have to say about this? Tune in tonight at ten. This is Kimberly Johnson reporting live from Trempealeau County."

There's a roar outside as the line of trucks start up and begin to move. The sound increases. I hear the front door open again and run to the window. There is Grandpa, without a coat, standing in front of the first truck, waving his arms. The wind gusts, and he brushes his wild gray hair from his face. The green truck, labeled "#127," starts to move forward. In a panic, I recall his words: *Over my dead body.* I tear out onto the front lawn. I call out, but Grandpa doesn't turn around.

"No, Grandpa, no!"

Instead of going around him, the huge truck skids, heading straight for him. Like the billion-year-old bluffs, Grandpa doesn't budge. There's no way I can get to him in time. My chest aches, and again I yell—but no sound comes out.

I jolt upright, awake, my heart pounding. I'm on the floor of my bedroom, tangled in blankets. Though dazed, it's clear I'm wearing the same clothes I had on last night. My arm is numb. I ache all over. In a panic, I push up my sleeve and the cuff of my pants. The bluish bruises on my legs, the cuts and scrapes on my arms, are all the confirmation I need. The battle *was* real. So I passed out from exhaustion and had a bad dream. No biggie. The experience of last night totally deserves one good nightmare. I'm actually happy to be removing thorns from my side. Comforting evidence. Raw knuckles, battle scars. At last, I turn over my hand. I'm jubilant. It's there, the mark.

The light streaming in tells me it's got to be close to noon. Reeling from last night's encounter with the sand monster, I stagger to my feet. Literally, I tumble toward the window. Raising the blinds, I have to grasp the windowsill to steady myself. The pane is completely iced over. A dozen spiral patterns face me. As they glimmer before my eyes, I reach out and press my palm to the coldness. The badgers. They'll be back.

I feel a tired smile breaking through when Grandpa John raps on my door. I grunt a greeting. He pokes his head in.

"By the way, Davie, the police rounded up those criminals last night. Three involved. Sittin' in jail sure as my coffee is brewin' in the kitchen. Want some?"

"Sure."

I give Grandpa a hug and follow him to the kitchen. Grandpa fills two mugs. My cup, "No Frac," he fills halfway. His cup, "Frac no!" gets filled to the top. Of course, I add milk all the way to the top. It's strange; just one sip seems to separate me from that awful nightmare—the man with the clipboard, the respirator, the trucks. Grandpa raises his mug, and we toast. Instantly I think back to the musta luminae fusing together. It's like me and Grandpa, in a way, thinking alike—being of the same mind.

I tiptoe into the den and see that Carl, Sharon, and Melissa are still passed out. Sharon lies on top of her sleeping bag with her jacket still on. Melissa, sprawled on the couch, is a vision with her white mohair headband and old olive army blanket.

Carl lies facedown, beached on the carpet. His head is turned to the side, his arms and legs sprawled as if he's flying. Yeah. Everything looks in order, more or less.

So I grab a pad and pencil, sit down at the kitchen table, and start making a list. Grandpa looks over my shoulder but doesn't say a thing. I come up with ways to spread the word, educate others, petition lawmakers, stage protests. We'll send out mailings, network, join with others—whatever it takes. There's no stopping, no backing down from this fight. Like badgers, we'll stand firm until someone takes notice. And like a spiral, our efforts—our journey—will continue on and on and on.

ACKNOWLEDGMENTS

I want to thank the following for their dedication to environmental protection and their spreading awareness of the continual need to stop, look, listen, and act in the interests of our earth. First and foremost, the Sierra Club, for creating a broad spectrum of environmental awareness and for decisive action. Kudos to Greenpeace and BadgerWatch, and to ecowatch.com for the following informative articles: "Mining Companies Invade Wisconsin for Frac Sand" (EcoNews, April 27, 2012) and "1,000 Healthcare Professionals Call on President Obama to Halt Fracking" (EcoNews, February 20, 2014).

Thanks also to the publishers of the following articles: "Frac Sand Mining Splits Wisconsin Communities" (the *Milwaukee-Wisconsin Journal Sentinel*); "Sand Mines in Wisconsin Unearth Environmental Problems" (the *Milwaukee Journal Sentinel*); "Wisconsin at 'Global Epicenter' of Frac and Sand Mining Industry" (the *Capital Times*); "Cuomo's fracking ban has some New York towns contemplating secession" (Yahoo! News, February 2015); "Fracking Confirmed as Cause of Rare 'Felt' Earthquake in Ohio" (*Seismological Society of America*, January 5, 2015); and "A Matter of Sand, Protesters gather at Interstate Bridge, March to Winona City Hall" (WinonaDailyNews. com, May 31, 2012).

Thanks to Jim Tittle for the 2013 documentary film *The Price of Sand*.

My appreciation to Kerry Magruder, Curator, History of Science Collections at the University of Oklahoma libraries, for permission to use the image of the Winter Hexagon.

My thanks to the Unitarian Universalist Fellowship of Winston

Salem for inspiring Earth Day and creating an invaluable community event; to TEEM, the environmental movement of Temple Emanuel of Winston Salem for hosting a series of films and speakers on timely environmental issues such as fracking.

A standing ovation goes to author, Naomi Klein, whose New York Times best-selling book and subsequent documentary, *This Changes Everything: Capitalism vs. Climate*, fueled the fire in my pen.

Special shout outs to Lois Miller for her generosity and fine photography; to Randall, an Auburn Tiger, a kind friend and kind of badger; to Cindy Wright, my writing friend and author, for patiently hearing me read chapters aloud (sometimes in characters' voices) and helpful feedback; and to positive and humorous Karen; to Winston Salem writers for welcoming me and cheering me on, which is very significant to my life as an author. My appreciation to my daughter, Haley—also a passionate writer—for understanding and believing in me; brother, Richard; and sister-in-law/friend, Lois, for listening to me talk, effervesce, and generally go on and on for a what seems like a long, long wonderful time. Thanks, Mom, for encouraging and valuing my creativity.

Finally, thanks to the little North Carolina store where I found a rare stuffed badger by accident, "Badge," who inhabits my cluttered study as my ecoconscience and my guide—badgering me to keep on task.

TOPICS FOR DISCUSSION

1. "Let wild be wild!" Discuss the meaning of Grandpa John's warning.

2. Why do you think the author titled the book *Ecowarriors*?

3. *The Bluffs of Baraboo* can be considered a *hybrid* genre, mixing fantasy and contemporary realism.

    What is your favorite use of *fantasy* in the book?

    What *real* issues are important to you?

4. Compare and contrast Melissa and Sharon. Find dialogue in the story to support your comments.

5. *To badger* is an idiom that means to persuade someone through stubborn persistence, repetition, or annoyance. How are badgers used as a positive symbol in the story?

6. Discuss the symbolism and importance of the Luna moth to the story.

7. Which character(s) do you personally relate to, and why?

8. The four Ecowarriors believe Wisconsin needs protection. Imagine what actions they will take together in the future.

9. In what ways does this book relate to your community? How can you and your friends join together to make a difference?

SUGGESTED READING

The Silent Spring, by Rachel Carson. Her efforts led to the ban on DDT, a highly toxic pesticide that threatened all wildlife.

Hoot, by Carl Hiaasen. In this humorous take on a serious subject, middle schoolers try to prevent the destruction of habitat and establish a preserve for endangered burrowing owls.

ACTIVITIES

* Research online articles on the environment. Before recycling the newspaper, clip eco-related articles from it. Paste them in a scrapbook or journal with the corresponding dates. Include nature-walk notes, photos, poems you write, songs that inspire you, drawings, a collage—even a cartoon.
* Contribute to your school newspaper. Write! When you're ready, try writing a letter to the editor of your town's local paper about topics that please or disturb you. Enlist your parents to help you; make it a family project.
* Get your family to join a *green* group such as your local chapter of the Sierra Club. They sponsor fun activities like hikes and outings.
* Plan a car-wash fundraiser with friends; donate the proceeds to an environmental cause.

COOL SITES

www.humanesociety.org—Teens receive training to become shelter volunteers. (The legal age requirement for volunteers is eighteen.)

www.epa.gov/high_school—A high school environmental center. Check out their cool Youtube channel. Learn about green living, recycling, climate change, and ecosystems.

www.Earthwatch.org—Expeditions designed for fifteen- to eighteen-years-olds provide hands-on opportunities to undertake vital, peer-reviewed scientific field research under the supervision of skilled research teams. Download a guide. Hike off-trail in national parks, or handle wild animals under guidance. Those under eighteen must be accompanied by a parent or guardian.

www.teensturninggreen.org—Read about a national, student-led movement and get informed about an eco-lifestyle through peer education and outreach programs. The Eco Top Chef program pairs middle school students with professional chefs.

www.dosomething.org—This website empowers youth to *be* the change they want to see in the world.

CPSIA information can be obtained at www.ICGtesting.com
Printed in the USA
LVOW06s0135061115

461327LV00003B/3/P

4/24